The Matchmaker

Dating the Divine: Book 1

Roxanne Gardener

Roxanne Gardener Designs

This is a work of fiction. Names, characters, places, and incidents either are the product of the author's imagination or are used fictitiously. Any resemblance to actual persons, living or dead, events, or locales is entirely coincidental.

Copyright © 2024 by Roxanne Gardener

All rights reserved. No part of this book may be reproduced or used in any manner without written permission of the copyright owner except for the use of quotations in a book review. For more information, address:

Info@roxannegardener.com

First paperback edition February 2024

Book Cover design by Casey Lees

ISBN 978-1-7779566-3-9 (Paperback)

ISBN 978-1-7779566-4-6 (Large print)

ISBN 978-1-7779566-2-2 (ebook)

www.roxannegardener.com

Contents

Prologue	1
Chapter 1	3
Chapter 2	9
Chapter 3	15
Chapter 4	21
Chapter 5	27
Chapter 6	29
Chapter 7	33
Chapter 8	35
Chapter 9	37
Chapter 10	43
Chapter 11	49
Chapter 12	51
Chapter 13	55
Chapter 14	59
Chapter 15	65

Chapter 16	69
Chapter 17	71
Chapter 18	77
Chapter 19	81
Chapter 20	89
Chapter 21	93
Chapter 22	97
Chapter 23	101
Chapter 24	105
Chapter 25	109
Epilogue	113
Get a Free Short Story	117
About the Author	119

Prologue

I'm not losing my mind. "Breathe. Just Breathe," I say to myself. It's done, I can't take it back. What I saw last night couldn't be real. I must have been hallucinating. As I feel the cold metal against my skin, I brace myself against the side of the elevator. *I will fix this*. We just need to talk, to sort things out. I need to stay calm.

The elevator made a ping noise. I was finally at his office, after what felt like hours. As the elevator doors open, I walk out and over to the posh-looking secretary behind the large desk. The secretary picks up the phone, and I overhear her saying "She's here". The door behind the desk opens and out walks someone I'm not expecting.

Who is she? Why is she in his office? The woman looks sleek and very annoyed. She is tall, blond, and looks to be in her thirties. Her floral blazer, black blouse, and jeans makes her look business casual. Her clothes look fresh and pressed, someone who took care to follow fashion trends. She has a huge pearl on a necklace, bigger than I'd ever seen or knew existed. Not exactly someone you'd expect to come out of the CEO's office. "Well, you have more gumption than I thought," she says with one hand on her hip.

Chapter 1

5 Weeks Earlier

Today is the day that changes everything. Excited about starting my new job, I dress up for my first day in a light pink blouse and white slacks and low black heels. My shoulder-length black hair is styled into a ponytail and my mahogany eyes are decorated with some pink eyeshadow and mascara. As it is still a little brisk outside, there was no need to use blush today. As I walk to work, I think about how difficult the interview had been.

Many people sought after my Marketing Research position, as it is at the prestigious matchmaking company called Matchmaker. The interview had been with a panel of eight interviewers from all over the company. Even the CEO had shown up. I conquered my nerves and presented myself like a boss. My presentation and answers to the questions left smiles on the panel's faces. With its lucrative salaries, benefits, and supportive environment, it is a top-ranking company to work at. There had been over a hundred candidates for my position and I couldn't believe they chose me!

I love how close to work I live and that I can take advantage of the good pleasant weather by walking to work. My path to work is a relaxing stroll through the downtown streets that have cherry trees blossoming. Cherry blossom trees are not common throughout Canada, but in Vancouver, they flourish and help mark the beginning of spring. Their white and pink varieties add a splash of color that is needed after the gloomy and wet winter on the Pacific West Coast.

As I am nearing the Matchmaker building just beside Burrard SkyTrain station, a subway system that goes below ground in downtown and above ground for most of the system and is about three stories in the sky, I walk through the cherry blossom trees surrounding the station. I walk slowly for a moment so I can enjoy the fully blooming flowers. I am feeling a little nervous about my first day, so I breath in the scent of the flowers and stretch my arms above my head to help calm me down. After a few minutes, I cross the street and go into the building.

The building houses a few different businesses, but they reserve the top two floors for Matchmaker. It even has amenities for all the employees of the building. There is a gym, hot tub, sauna, and cafeteria. I can't wait to use the gym and hot tub for free. I no longer need to pay for a gym membership and can save that money for an extra meal out on weekends with friends. I hope my new workmates are pleasant and it would be great to eat in the cafeteria with them. Beside the building is a waterfall feature that is a great place to relax and enjoy some fresh air on breaks. It is an ideal location, and I am excited to work here.

Taking a deep breath and walking into the building, the elevator is already open on the ground floor, so I take it up to the office. I walk up to the secretary and introduce myself to her, "hi I'm Janan Candemir. It's my first day here." The secretary welcomes me and shows me to my desk. She also has her red hair in a ponytail. Her purple blouse, gray skirt, and black flats compliment her green eyes. She looks like a professional who takes pride in her work. "You will love working for Matchmaker. We are very supportive here. If there is anything you need, just ask!"

"Thanks, I appreciate it." I say as the bubbly secretary smiles and walks back to her desk.

My desk is stationed next to a window, and there are three other desks in the enclave. There are two facing one wall, with the other two facing the opposite wall. My desk mates are a middle-aged man, a young man, and a young woman.

CHAPTER 1

The young woman is the one who shares the wall with me. At thirty, I am still considered a youngish woman and I hope to get along with my teammates who seem to be about my age. They all smile at me and we make our introductions. "Welcome Janan! Take your time to get settled in. You will meet with our supervisor in a bit and she'll show you the ropes. I'm Anne and this is Philip and Max. We usually have lunch together if you'd like to join us?" the young woman says. She has brown eyes and short brown hair in a bob, which made her look younger than she is. The young man is Max. He has green eyes and red hair that curl on top of his hair in a flourish that makes him look younger. Philip has black hair with little gray spots and a small balding spot on the back of his head. While he is put together nicely, you can tell he is worn out and tired looking, as his clothes are rumpled and well used and his eyes look exhausted.

"That sounds lovely," I reply as I sit at my desk and adjust the chair to my level, and put my purse away into a drawer in the desk. I go to sign into my computer but then remember I don't have that set up yet. I can hear my desk mates clacking away on their keyboards.

Luckily, my supervisor comes strolling in not too long afterward. She has brown eyes and an angel bob and wears a black blazer over a white blouse with orange flowers on it and black pants and black low heels. She radiates authority and professionalism. "Welcome Janan! I'm Amanda and I assume your teammates already introduce themselves?"

I nod my head.

"Great, I'll give you the tour, and then we can set up your accounts with IT". We tour the office, and I like the little kitchenette and espresso machine, knowing I would use both regularly. Luckily, it isn't too far from my desk either, so I can easily grab a coffee or snack. IT gives me my temporary passwords, so I can get set up on my desk. Amanda then brings me to the small meeting room where she briefs me on my role, expectations, and where the team is on their current projects. I feel invigorated by learning about my role and projects and can't wait to start. The highest priority project is one about trying to find bottlenecks or points along the customer journey that decrease the level of customer satisfaction. We want to make the customer experience more easy to use.

I fall into the rhythm of my new role quickly and enjoy my first few days at work. Taking lunch with my coworkers lets me get to know them and feel part of the team. I take my coffee breaks outside by the waterfall feature, enjoying the sound of the water and the sunlight.

A week into my new job, my coworkers and I go to a nearby pub after work. We leave a little early to get there for happy hour and to get a seat before the pub gets too busy. We each order an appetizer and a drink. I get chicken wings with a rye and diet coke, my favorite pub combo.

"So how do you like Matchmaker, Janan?" asks Philip as he takes a bite of his slider.

"Oh, so far, so good. You guys have been great at catching me up on the projects. Everyone is so welcoming and friendly here."

"Pardon my asking, but are you single or in a relationship?" asks Max, looking at me directly, making me feel uncomfortable.

"I'm single," I reply half-heartedly, not wanting to answer. Feeling that slightly guarded feeling that you get when you're a thirty-year-old woman who is single and gets asked that question.

"That's great that you work for Matchmaker then! You can use the service for free as an employee, did you know?" Anne replies excitedly. "We can help you find suitable candidates if you like."

"She doesn't need the matchmaking service yet. She just started here. Give her some time to get to know the people she works with first." Replies Max, who spoke while looking at the floor, his cheeks red.

"Oh, we should share a bit more about ourselves. How about we go around the group and talk about ourselves a little?" Anne proposes.

CHAPTER 1

We agree, and I find out a bit about everyone. Philip is married, and he likes role-playing in a Dungeons and Dragons game. Living with a four-month-old baby at home, explains his exhausted look. Max is single and into AI, so he knows all about all the AI developments that are in the news. Anne is in a relationship with a woman she met through Matchmaker. They have been together for two years now. She also enjoys sewing her own clothes and loves rompers. And then there is me, single and into Latin dancing, even though I just started and am not that good yet. I have only started mastering the basics.

As we wrap up after a few more drinks and chatting, we get ready to leave. As Philip and Anne have others to rush home to, Max and I are the last ones out the door. "Can I walk you home Janan?" Max asks quietly, shifting from foot to foot.

"Oh, thank you, Max, but I don't live far. I'll be fine. See you next week." I say with a smile and wave as I walk away. I'm not sure if he is interested, but I don't want to date a man I work with. Things would become messy or uncomfortable quickly at work if we broke up.

Starting my second week on the job, while on my break by the waterfall feature, a middle-aged man comes towards me and stands beside me. He has brown eyes and a buzz cut with his black hair. He wears a white Oxford shirt with brown pants and black loafers. From his posture, he radiates a sense of authority, like he is in the military. As he stands beside me he says, "Hi Janan, I'm Landon. I work for Matchmaker too. I work with management. Is it alright if I chat with you for a few minutes?" I see his lanyard and that he is telling the truth about working for Matchmaker, so I relax and allow him to sit beside me.

"How are you settling in at Matchmaker?" he asks.

"Oh, I am getting the hang of things here. My desk mates are great and they have helped me get up to date quickly. They caught me up on the projects and I could jump in right away."

"That's great to hear." He looks at me with a determination which makes me realize he is here for a specific purpose. This is not a friendly chat.

"I have a client," he begins, "who would love to meet you. He thinks you are a perfect match. But he is a little unorthodox, though." Landon pauses for a moment.

Unorthodox? What does that mean? Many questions pop into my head. What kind of man is he? Why does he want to meet me? What did I do to get his attention? Who is this guy?

Landon continues, "He would like to meet you for supper at a restaurant where you have your meal in the dark. Have you ever gone to one before?"

Why does he want a blind first date? Is he afraid of what I might think of his physical appearance? I guess this blind date would truly be blind, at least for me.

"No, I haven't been to one before." I take a drink of my coffee to calm my nerves.

He continues, "He says he wants you to get to know him before seeing him. A little like the TV show Love is Blind, do you know it? Would you be interested?"

I won't lie and say it did not intrigue me, as I am single and had just signed up for the free matchmaking service at my job. But that is fast for a match, as I had just signed up. I think it is strange to meet someone in the dark, but I am a fan of Love is Blind. After a moment of thinking, I say, "I think I'll give it a shot. At the least, it could be a great networking opportunity." Landon is happy and says he'd message me the details of the time and place and he leaves me alone to enjoy the rest of my break. As I finish my coffee, I wonder what the man is interested in but can't meet me normally. He must be some kind of eccentric person, or maybe he has something he wants to hide. I have trouble guessing which it is, but I think I'd still try it. There is nothing wrong with having a conversation with someone, even if it is in the dark. What do I have to lose? Plus, it would be in a public place, so I'd be safe, but I am worried about what this man is trying to hide from me.

Chapter 2

A few days later I am Ubering to the location of my mysterious date. Within 10 minutes, my Uber brings me to the restaurant, a well-known restaurant in Vancouver in the Kitsilano neighborhood. Known locally as Kits, it is a laid-back neighborhood that is known for its giant outdoor saltwater pool, the longest outdoor swimming pool in North America, Kits Beach which is one of the top ten city beaches in the world, and trendy restaurants and shops along fourth avenue. I am wearing a nice black maxi dress even though he won't see it. I still want to dress up, as it makes me feel more confident and sexy. My jet black hair is loose around my shoulders with large soft curls that took me an hour to make it look just right. The curls flow around me and I feel like I'm ready for the red carpet. My makeup is minimal, just enough to make me look polished. I have highlighted my eyes with some eyeliner and mascara with neutral olive eyeshadow to match my skin. I stare into my compact mirror. "You got this girl!" I say to myself. Feeling pumped about the night, I feel prepared for whatever might happen. And looking this good, I feel prepared if he wants to meet face to face, after we finish eating in the dark. I hope we get along and can meet properly after dinner. I'm not just curious about what he's like, I'm also very curious about what he looks like. This suspense of going in blind is adding more nervousness and excitement than my usual first dates. It's been a while since I've felt like this and I think it's a good sign.

I get out of the Uber and walk to the entrance of the restaurant. "Hi, I'm Janan and I'm meeting a date here. Do you know if he has arrived already?"

The maitre'd replies enthusiastically "Oh yes, we are expecting you! He has already arrived. It's funny that you guys are meeting here for a blind date. It's truly blind! Have you been here before?" I shook my head no. "Well, you will have a dining experience like you never had before with our special menu of the day. You're not allergic to anything, are you? Or have any dietary restrictions?" Feeling a little overwhelmed by this news, I pull myself together. "I'm picky with seafood, but can otherwise eat anything." I remind myself that the staff and other patrons will be in the restaurant so we won't be alone.

The maitre'd guides me into the restaurant to the table and as I feel for the chair to sit down, I hear him speak, "Hi Janan. Thank you for agreeing to meet me," says a man with a resonating timbre from across the table. *Oh, that's a nice accent. This is off to a good start.* "and for understanding my desire to meet you sight unseen. I promise I am not a creepy guy. We have met briefly in the past and who I am would surprise you, but not disappoint you. But who I am and where we've met will stay a secret for now."

I can't place the voice to anyone I know, so he must be someone I only know socially or from my work history. "Well, this is certainly something I haven't done before. Luckily, I'm also a fan of Love is Blind and thought this could be an interesting experience," I reply.

He lightly laughs. "I'm glad you aren't against this idea. Let's enjoy our dinner and get to know one another."

"Do you know what's on the menu for this evening? Or is it a surprise to us both?" I inquire, letting myself relax into the conversation.

"We can have only so many surprises at once, so I'll tell you what we are eating. We will have a three-course meal: pumpkin soup, asparagus and steak with a mushroom sauce, and a strawberry basil dessert soup. A low-carb meal. I like to follow a keto diet."

"Oh, delicious. I'm not on any diet myself, but I try not to eat too many processed sugar foods. So my carbs are usually low as well. I go to the gym three times a week and exercise at home two days a week. It's good to keep fit, not necessarily to look good, but to be healthier. I used to be a little on the heavier side for a few years and I noticed the difference when eating well and working out. The energy level is so much better on a low-sugar diet."

"That's great to hear that you value your health. We can easily dine together then and maybe work out together at the gym. I used to go to the YMCA."

"Oh, me too, but now I go to the gym at work. That would be funny if we had run into each other there, but didn't know it."

"I would have remembered you any time we may have crossed paths, Janan. You're not forgettable."

"I guess," I laugh softly. "Men hit on me at the gym, but the ones I've dated rarely go on more than one date with me. My personality doesn't fit my shy look. I know you've met me before and hopefully, you have a better view of my personality. I am frank and some people don't like it."

"No, please be yourself," he reassures me. "I have seen you in the real world and from what I see, your personality is one of a strong and confident woman. I prefer women who are authentic, that don't hold back, can stand on their own, and know how to ask for what they want."

"Wow," I breathe out. "That's such a nice compliment. I wish I could tell you something nice, but I can't place you by your voice. You have me at a disadvantage."

With a smile in his voice, he replies, "Yes, I have the advantage. But I hope you would like to get to know me more and maybe one day you can repay the compliment. For now, let's enjoy this meal and our great conversation."

We eat the appetizer talking about our interests and hobbies. We laugh while we are talking about funny stories from our younger years while eating our main meal. As dessert is ending, we talk about our past dating and relationship stories.

"I know I'm unconventional, but I have had problems dating when I am open about who I am. I've tried dating this way and it seems to work best because I can completely be myself without holding back. Though I rarely go past the first date as I am looking for that special someone. But you Janan are a wonder and I'd love to see where things may go. Are you up for it?"

"Yes, I think we get on well with each other and I would like that chance to get to know you more." I say as I lean towards him.

"Great! I was a little scared there that you might not want to keep dating," he replies and takes a deep breath. "Well, there's one more thing I'd like to run by you. I'd like to continue this dating-in-the-dark experience a little longer. Would you be willing to continue meeting in the dark for a month? To see where this goes? We can get to know each other more deeply this way."

I think about it. It is a very weird request, but I have enjoyed his company up to this point. He sees me much more clearly than my past dates have for quite some time. I hesitate. Would this be too weird? Deciding in an instant to trust my gut, I reply, "Yes, let's keep dating. But could I at least have your name?"

"You can call me Eros. And thank you for entrusting me with this request."

"Eros, like the god of love?"

"Yes, exactly," he says warmly. "You say my name so nicely. Are you up to meeting me tomorrow? I'd ideally like to meet you a few hours every day, if that is possible."

Why does he want to meet every day? And in the dark? I feel a little uncomfortable with having so many questions, but I like him so far. Feeling a yearning I haven't felt before, I know I want to get to know this man. There is some force pulling me towards him as I am leaning over the edge of the table toward his voice. I want this man. "I guess we are on a timeline! Sure, let's meet."

"Great, I'll send you the information tomorrow."

The maitre'd shows me outside. "That sounded like a great date," the waiter comments. "I'm so excited for you. Remember to come back here on your anniversary. Good luck!"

I laugh a "thank you" to the maitre'd as I get into my Uber to go home.

On my ride home, I can't believe how the night has progressed. Who is this man? He seems like a catch, but why isn't he taken already? Is there something wrong with him, I can't seem to pick up any red flags? His stories of past dates made it clear he is an important and popular man who has to worry about his image and other people's intentions toward him. I sigh, hoping my instincts were reliable. I want to give this man a chance. He is the first man in a long time to get me interested in hoping for something meaningful to come out of it. This experiment of dating in the dark can be something that works for me as well. Men are not the only ones to get caught up in physical appearances. This way of dating might help me learn about this man more deeply, as we would rely heavily on communication. From his seductive voice, I feel like he is a handsome man, and I would like to not get caught up in his looks. I want to find a love that is deep, not superficial anyway, and maybe this way of dating would help that goal. Though he knows who I am, it isn't as fair. But the dark does emphasizes our conversation more than relying on appearance. We would get to know each other equally by focusing on sharing our thoughts, feelings, history, and goals. I want to do this. I feel excited by the novel idea.

Chapter 3

The next morning, I get ready for work and the promise of seeing Eros at our date after work. Even though we wouldn't see each other, I want to look nice. I humm as I get ready, excited by what the day could bring. I wear my hair down around my shoulders and put on a burgundy red romper.

At lunch, I eat with my coworkers, as I have fallen into the habit of doing. "What's got you so excited, Janan? You are humming full of energy today! And you look nice in your romper! I love rompers if you haven't guessed, I wear them a lot," Anne asks, laughing. She has one on today as well, a nice navy blue romper with white dots.

"Oh, I had a great date last night and I'm seeing him again tonight."

"Isn't that a little fast to see him again?" Max asks worriedly, with a heart-wrenching look.

"It was a great date! I haven't been on this good a date in a long time, even if it was unconventional."

"What do you mean, unconventional?" asks Anne.

"Oh, we met at a restaurant where we had dinner in the dark. We couldn't see each other. Have you ever tried it? The food is fabulous!" I say with a wide grin.

"You mean you don't know what he looks like at all? How can you trust this man? What's he hiding? Is he married?" Max questions with a soft but firm voice.

"I don't think he is lying about anything, so he wouldn't be married. Sure, I don't know what he looks like, but we get on well together and isn't that more important?"

"I think what we are all saying, Janan, is that we are worried for you and hope it works out. Do you know when you'll get to meet him properly?" Philip asks.

"I will see him face to face in a month," I say softly. I know it is unconventional, but I wasn't expecting this powerful reaction. They barely know me, but I know they just want to look out for me. "Don't worry, I won't be unsafe, I'm taking precautions," I reassure my coworkers.

Nearing the end of my workday, I was feeling a little low. My excitement has dimmed a bit by how my coworkers responded to my dating situation. I want to trust Eros, but I know I have to keep rational during this experience. I look at my phone and his instructions for where to meet. It is nearby, so I walk over. I look at the building. It is a condo building...I ring the buzzer, wondering why we are meeting here. Landon answers the buzzer "Hi Janan, great to talk with you again. Eros isn't here yet. He wants you to look at the apartment before he gets here, so you'll feel safe."

I have to admit; I am feeling far from safe, but having Landon here reassures me, as I know we work together and I could call the police at anytime if anything goes wrong. I had looked him up on the company database and saw that he works in upper management as an assistant to the vice president, Zoe Lennon. But just in case, before heading up the elevator, I text my sister the address of where I am. My sister confirms she'll call me in an hour just to make sure I am safe.

When I enter the condo, I see that someone expertly decorated it in a minimalist modern style, which is my favorite style. Landon happily shows me around the condo. "Don't worry, if you ever feel uncomfortable, just say so and Eros will understand and do whatever you need him to do, even leave if necessary," he reassures me. "But the lights will turn off at eight pm when Eros arrives. They will not turn on until the next morning. So if you would like to, you can wait in the living room, which is also close to the front door, so you can leave easily if you feel uncomfortable."

I feel reassured and sit down on the couch in the living room. I see a bottle of white wine open on the table with two glasses and a platter of cheese and meat. My sister Chloe calls, and I tell her where I am, and that I feel safe, and I show her around the condo through video chat.

"Wow! What a nice condo! Not that you'll enjoy it being in the dark. Are you sure about doing this?" Chloe worries. I reassure her and say that I will call her when I leave. I go back to the couch to wait.

The lights go off at eight pm sharp. I jump a little on the couch and wait with a fast-beating heart. I am both a little nervous and excited as I hear the door handle click open. Eros calls out "Hi Janan, it's me Eros! I'm just coming in the door."

I laugh, of course, Eros is being overly cautious for me to be comfortable. "Thanks for the fair warning Eros," I reply. "I'm sitting on the couch in the living room."

Hearing Eros walk slowly to the living room and over to the chair opposite the couch, I feel more excitement as he sits near me. "Ouff made it without hurting myself," he says, laughing. "So, is this weird or what? But it works, trust me."

My mood lifts, and I release the pent-up stress I had been holding onto while waiting. "Yes, it is weird and people are worried for me, but I feel like I can trust you. Please don't disappoint me."

"I will do everything I can to make you feel safe. Whenever you feel uncomfortable, scared, or just off let me know and I'll do whatever you ask, even leave. You are in control. What you say goes."

"Thank you."

"How about we dig into this wine and charcuterie board?"

We laugh as Eros tries to pour the wine into the cup. Even though I can't see him, he makes loud noises as he keeps getting his hands wet from pouring the wine. He tells me he was coming with the wine. His hand is outstretched, and he sounds so close, so I put my hand out in the air and try to find the glass. After a few seconds, I find the glass and take it out of his hand. I try it and it's a cool and smooth pinot-gris. We eat and drink while talking about our arrangement.

"I would like to propose an agreement for us to date this month," Eros begins.

"What kind of agreement? Don't we already have one?"

"I would like to propose that we meet every night this month here in this condo. I will come to visit from 8 pm to 11 pm. You can stay here as it's closer to work if you'd like. I will leave as promised at 11 every night so you can have the place to yourself."

"That's a lot of dates! But I guess we only have one month. What happens after the month?"

"No matter how we end up, I will introduce myself to you in the light. You deserve to see who you've been dating. If it all goes well, I would like us to become an official couple. And I would like us to live together as well. Of course, this is if you agree."

"Well, it will be nice to meet you properly. I like that part a lot. If we both like each other, I'd agree to become a couple. But living together might be too soon. I think we need to come back to that later on. As for meeting you every night, I have a life, you know! Like seeing family and friends, and going to the gym. I think we don't need to meet every day."

"I hear you and understand. I don't want you to change your life, but I would like to give this a real shot and I believe for one month, if we can commit to seeing each other every day, we will build a strong connection."

"How about during the week we see each other and on weekends I can see my friends and family?"

"That sounds like a suitable compromise. Let's try that for the first week and see how we both feel. Remember, if you want to stop, you just have to tell me, ok?"

"I don't plan on staying here. I feel better going home after our dates."

CHAPTER 3

"I understand. If you want to go home, please let me have Landon drive you home just to be safe. And if you ever want to stay, the option is still available for you."

"It's not that far, really. I prefer to walk home. But thank you for your concern." I say, while leaning back on the couch.

"I like how you're independent, but I hope you'll let me take care of you as well. I want to support and protect you."

"Thanks, I appreciate it, but it might take me some time to rely upon you, as I have a habit of taking care of myself. And I haven't found someone I felt I could lean on yet. Hopefully, you'll be different."

We finish the bottle of wine and the charcuterie board. "Oh, look, it's almost 11 pm. We should make our way home. I will leave first. Please give me 10 minutes before you head out. I look forward to seeing you tomorrow."

I drink the last sip of my wine and reply, "I had fun tonight. I'm interested in seeing where this goes. Have a good night."

"Goodnight," Eros says as he walks towards the door. He walks slowly to make sure he hits nothing.

As the door closes behind him, I take out my phone and call my sister. Chloe is relieved that I had a good time, but she is worried about the arrangement.

"Why can't you see who he is until the end of the month? What if he just disappears? How can you trust him? What if he's a married man trying to find a mistress? What if he is part of a sex ring and he is luring you in?"

"I trust him enough to try it out. I will be cautious and take my time to get to know him. You know where I am and I've given you Landon's contact information, so if something happens, you can go to the police with it. So there is very little risk that something bad will happen."

"Are you sure he will not look down on you? Or bully you into doing what he wants? Or has weird fetishes? Like this dating in the dark arrangement?"

I sigh quietly. "You shouldn't be thinking the worst of him just because we are dating sight unseen. He is a normal person, you know. Besides, he reassures me I am in control of this experiment and he will listen to me. There's nothing really to worry about."

"Well, I am concerned for you. I don't think you should do this."

"Thank you for your concern, but I want to try it, so I will." Ending the call with her, I walk towards the door, as I am sure I'd been on the phone longer than 10 minutes. Exiting the building, I have a short refreshing walk home in the cool spring breeze of spring. I am still excited by the thought of Eros, even though I worry a little about what the catch is. Why does he feel he has to hide who he is? I get home and go to bed smiling, thinking of our conversation. But I have a worry in the back of my head, that doesn't go away, that I need to be cautious.

Chapter 4

I spend every weeknight with Eros for that week. I find him charming, confident, and amusing. That Friday at lunch, my coworkers ask how my dating life is going. "Are you still seeing that guy who wants to date you in the dark?" Anne asks.

"Yes, I am. It's going well. We get along so well. He's quite the conversationalist."

Max asks, "Have you met him properly yet?"

"No, but that's part of the fun. You really pay attention to what someone is saying when that's all you have to rely on."

"What? How could you be into it? He's lying to you, I'm sure of it! He must be married!" Max says, gripping his coffee cup.

"Thanks for your concern, but it's not any of your business. It's between him and me." Getting up, I pack my things. "I'll eat somewhere else today." Leaving the lunchroom, I go to eat by the waterfall feature outside the building. I need its soothing noise to calm me down. Tonight, I resolve I need to know more about who he is.

After work I go to the gym, needing to work out some of my stress, I stay longer than normal. After my shower at the gym, I get ready to meet Eros. Walking over to Eros' condo, I wonder where he lives, since it's obviously not the condo we are using. It would be something I'd have to ask him, along with a lot of other questions tonight. I am enjoying myself, but my sister and coworkers are right; I need to know him much better and I need to know more personal information about his life.

Sitting in the dark condo, I think about what I want to know about Eros. How do you really get to know someone? Favorite color? Hobbies? Your job? But what about things that take longer to learn, like temperament and affection style? I want to get to know Eros more, but I struggle to focus on what questions really matter. Sitting in the dark staring at the floor that I can't see, I focus on my determination to find answers tonight, then as I hear the handle and squeak of the door, my heart beats faster and my stomach knots.

"Janan?" Eros calls from the door to the living room.

"Yes, I'm here on the couch on the left side, like usual."

"Oh, I thought maybe you weren't here today since the lights weren't on earlier. I'm really glad you're here."

"I came earlier than normal, so had the dusk of the day to get myself settled."

"You sound different." Eros pauses beside the couch. "Is everything ok?"

"Eros…I think we need to have a more serious talk today. People I know are worried about me and with reason. This is a strange way to date someone. I need to get to know you better. But I don't know what I need to ask to do that. I feel like I need to ask you questions that are deeper than the usual questions on a date, but I don't know where to start," I say in an aggravated voice.

"I'm happy to answer anything you want to know. I want us to get to know each other really well. Please feel free. If you don't know where to start, I can just talk about myself a little and you can direct the conversation."

"Thank you for understanding my needs. Can I … can I hold your hand?" I ask, needing to feel connected.

CHAPTER 4

Eros moves toward the side of the couch and sits down next to me. "Here, let me find your hand." He skims his hands along the edge of the couch until they hit my knee. I reach down to his hand and brush it over his. I feel his left hand and don't feel a ring. *Well, that's good. He's not married then*, I think. He turns over his hand, and we intertwine our fingers. Feeling his smooth hands, there's a little sense of electricity that skitters across my skin. I could feel his heat, his energy, flowing through my hand and up my arm to my chest. What was this feeling? I'd never felt this connection with anyone before. Is this energy from Eros? Or is this my body feeling a deep desire for him? Whatever this feeling is, I like it. It makes me feel more alive than I have before.

"Where should I start? Well, I work at a company where I am passionate about my job. I work a lot but that doesn't mean I don't find time to be with family and friends. I value your time and would spend a lot of time with you. Spending quality time is one of my top love languages. While I look like I'm thirty-five, I'm older than that. I love animals but don't have one at the moment, as I spend my free time being busy learning, being active, doing archery, and cooking. I enjoy cooking new recipes and I'm known for showing up at family and friends' places with a new dish I've tried making. You could say acts of service are my second top love language. I am a calm person, but I get excited by food! I am financially sound and I live a life without excess, yet I spend money on things that save me time or bring me joy."

"Have you ever been married, and do you have any children?" I quietly ask.

"Well, a long time ago, in another life, I was married, and we had a child. My child is so caring and loves to make people happy. She's an adult now and I think you would get along with her. You are both such independent women. You can meet her if you like, once this month is over."

"I'm honored you want me to meet your daughter. But how do you have an adult daughter? Where is her mother? Where do you live? You don't live here, do you?"

"I married very young and unfortunately, my wife died a long time ago. I don't live here. It's a friend's place, they are away on vacation and are allowing me to use it. I live downtown as well, close to the library in Yaletown."

"I'm sorry for your loss. It must have been hard on you and your daughter. Oh, that's a great location. I enjoy living in the West End with all the unique homes in the area. It's a great neighborhood." His hand squeezes my hand slightly.

"Thanks. It was hard for a long time, but because we had each other, my daughter and I, we got through it. I'm not very close to my family. We are all over the place, but I attempt to make sure my daughter knows she's loved. It's great that we live close to each other. It will make dating easier." He says with a warmth in his voice.

"Are you famous or something? Is that why you are worried about me seeing you?"

"I'm not famous in the way you think. The paparazzi don't care about me, if that's what you're wondering. I am well known in business terms, but nothing that would make me famous. But if you were to see me, you would know me at once as we have met before. I know this is unorthodox, but I believe this experiment of dating in the dark will be a good place to start our relationship. It will give us a solid foundation to stand on when we bring our relationship out in the open. I tried this once before, it was how my late wife and I dated and it was great for our relationship. I believe we will also make a great couple, so I wanted to try this experiment again with you."

"This experiment is interesting, but why are you so sure that it will work? It only worked for you one time before. What about all the opportunities since then that you passed on because of this test?"

"Believe me, you learn a lot about someone through this experiment. More than you would through normal dating. Already, I see your inquisitive side and your straight to the point attitude."

"I'm having a harder time getting to know you, it seems. You answer my questions, but don't go into full details. What are you afraid that I'll learn?"

"I want you to know everything about me, but some things will take some time to explain. If I say I am the actual god Eros and have lived for five thousand years, would you believe me or think I'm nuts?"

"I would think you're laughing at me."

"Exactly, so I must go slow to let you learn about me." He says, squeezing my hand, "many details of my life are extraordinary and others are normal. So I will share the normal with you and let you know the extraordinary, when you're ready, I will start telling you more."

"I guess I will have to see if we are compatible or if you are leading me on. I don't like this uncertainty about you."

"I know. Thank you for trying. I really want you to learn more about me, but it needs to be slow."

Chapter 5

Deciding to get to the bottom of this relationship, I ask Eros "What made you decide you wanted to date me?"

Eros seems to get energized by this question, like he can't wait to share. "The first time I saw you up close, you were so confident and passionate. It grabbed my attention right away. I saw you do a presentation and loved how you handled yourself and the audience."

"How were you there for that?" I interrupt him.

"I was part of the audience and you were magnificent." He says elusively. "And before that I saw you out in the real world helping those less fortunate. I came across an event you planned to raise support for orphans. Your passion for helping orphans feel loved by volunteers and also for helping to support them in finding families is awe-inspiring."

"I know what it's like for those kids. I'm an orphan myself. But I am lucky to have a younger sister to feel connected to. And an uncle and aunt who stepped in to watch over us even though we were adults when my parents passed away. But, enough about me. Do you have any causes you care about?"

"I have several. Such as, I believe everyone has a right to information that can help them improve their lives or feel part of the community, which is why I support libraries. I also believe that everyone should have access to food and homes, so I help at shelters and food banks for the homeless. Also, I support programs for halfway homes. I've seen how hard life is when disaster strikes. I've seen many people become homeless and starving, and I like to do as much as I can to help. By providing support for the homeless and providing them with community spaces where they can feel part of the community, we can hopefully turn their lives around."

I feel like we are on the same wavelength. Not going to lie, but hearing him talk about his causes makes me turned on. I believe we are both looking out for those in need, and it makes me feel more connected to him. I want to know more about this man.

"How come you didn't come and introduce yourself at the time?" I ask as I pull his hand closer to me.

"I didn't want to interrupt your time with the kids. They seemed to be all over you."

"Oh, I see. How did you come to hit on me then through Landon then?"

"Well, I was going through Matchmaker's website and came across your profile. Knowing you were single and looking for a partner, I wanted to get your attention before someone else got it. I didn't want to lose my chance with you."

"That's not fair. You've seen me many times, and I know little about you. Could I see your profile, without the picture, of course? I feel like I should also interview you just as much as you are interviewing me."

"I'll send it right away. Why didn't I think of that? Sorry, you are right, it's only right that you get the same information about me from my profile." He squeezes my hand in apology, "the first thing I'll do on Monday is send you my profile."

"Thank you. I look forward to seeing it."

"But you know, I'll answer any question you have, so feel free and ask away."

Chapter 6

"Is there anything you're very nerdy about?" I say as I lean in closer to him.

"There's this game I love. It's called Tabula. But no one plays it anymore except my family. I used to play it all the time. The closest game to it nowadays is backgammon."

"Backgammon!" I laugh. "That's for old people. No one plays that anymore. What's Tabula then?"

"I can teach you, if you'd like to learn."

"Sure, old man," I continue to laugh.

"Hey, I told you I was older. I bet you'll like it once I teach you."

"I can try it." I pull his hand closer. I really want to get closer to him.

"It's a date then. We will play it once the month is over."

We sit in silence as I try to think of other things to ask. It is a calm silence, not an uncomfortable silence. I'm so curious I have trouble settling on a question. He sounds like an old person, but his hands are smooth like a young person. I'm not worried about how old he is. I just want to get to know him more.

"What kind of lover are you?" I ask, thinking of typical dating questions.

"I am an attentive lover. I make sure I see to the needs of my lover. My third love language is words of affirmation. I like to hear how good a lover I am. And I tell my lover how much they mean to me verbally. You will always know what you mean to me, as I will tell you every day how special you are to me." I feel something release in me with these words. I feel like I could trust him with my heart, for the first time in my life I feel this way with a man. No guy has made me feel as secure as Eros. He continues, "I like nicknames for lovers a lot. I guess I can be very cheesy. Tell me Janan, what kind of lover are you?"

Struggling to find my voice as I feel waves of desire and warmth from inside me at the knowledge that I can trust a man to stay and love me, I center myself from our connected hands. I finally find my voice and answer, "I value quality time together. Time together is very important to me, as we never know how much time we have with someone before they leave or die."

Thinking for a moment about my parents, feeling their loss. "I don't know what kind of lover I am as I haven't been in a long-term relationship yet, as the guys I date don't stay around very long. I like to think of myself as a very supportive partner, helping my partner reach their goals."

"We will build our relationship in time. There is no rush. We have all the time we could need. Just be present with me and let me know if there are any issues you have. Your frankness about issues will be great for open communication." He reassures me, "Don't be afraid to be yourself. That is who I'm here to meet, you, all of you. I'm not going anywhere."

This man says all the right things. I'm falling for him hard. I want to know him fully, spirituality and physically. Wanting to do more than just hold his hand, I want to please him and myself. But I'm worried that this is too fast. That even though he says these wonderful things, he'll disappear like everyone else does. The only person I can count on is my sister. Everyone else leaves, willing or not. It scares me to trust him. But his words calm me down. I want to try.

He senses my inner turmoil and says, "it's OK. Take your time. We have all night. Thankfully, it's a Friday, so we don't need to worry about work in the morning." He cups my hand in both of his, "What are your goals Janan? What gets you up in the morning?"

Even though it feels like an interview question, it helps me center myself. "Well, I want to run a team of market researchers, have a successful partnership with my husband, have a kid, and travel more. Nothing unexpected. You know the usual goals."

"I think you can think even bigger than that. I think you could do so much more. What would you do if you didn't have to worry about money or time?"

"I don't know, honestly. I've never thought of it. I guess I'd help the orphans more. See the world more."

"What if you had special powers? What powers would you like to have?"

"I would like powers that help people. Definitely not hearing what's inside people's heads. I think that would make me go crazy. Maybe powers to bring people together so they'd stop fighting. What power would that be? Team synergy?"

"That's an interesting power. You know, some people say love can bring people together. It's the ultimate power."

"I think it can bring people together but also divide people as some get it and some don't. There's usually a hurt party in love. Unless they're polyamorous, I guess."

"That's an interesting take on love. There are people who get hurt, but usually they find the right love later with the right partner. I agree not everyone can have their first choice as it might be the wrong person for them and they don't know it. But when you find that person, there's no stopping the power of love."

"You should come work for my company! They'd love to have someone like you. I bet you'd be able to work in upper management. But then I couldn't date you, I don't date men I work with. It always gets so messy."

"I'll keep that in mind." He laughs then says "you are so special to me Janan. I will figure out a way for both of us. Just let me take care of you."

"What do you mean?"

"You'll see later. Just don't worry about us dating."

"Ok. Now I am a little worried."

"I got you. I'll take care of it."

"Ok," I say as I pull away from him a little. I don't like this taking care of it mentality that he showed. I like to control myself.

"Normally I don't like this controlling manner, but since I'm out of the loop about what it is you need to control, I'm going to trust you. Please don't disappoint me."

"Sorry, I can be a little controlling. I just want to take care of you, not control you, I promise. I like to be in control of situations and this one I can take care of with a little finesse. But it might take some time before I can completely fix the situation to your liking. So please trust me to take care of it."

I swallow and think about it. I do not know what he's going to fix, but it's to keep us together, so I'll try to trust him. For now, at least. I will wait and see what it's about. At least he's being honest about there being a potential problem to fix. I sigh deeply and smell his cologne. Oh, what a great smell. It was Hugo Boss's cologne Boss. My favorite cologne. How did he know? I want to press myself against him and smell him. This man knows how to get me wet without touching him. How does he do it?

Chapter 7

Pulling myself out of the sexual haze that was surrounding me, I ask, "Please tell me more about your family. You said you weren't close. Why is that?"

He sighs, "Well it's not that we aren't close per se, it's more that we've lived close together for such a long time and that we need space from each other's personalities, so we are in contact with each other but don't see each other regularly. The only exception to this is my daughter and my mother. We are a close-knit unit. We work together on various projects. But we also keep to ourselves sometimes so we don't get sick of each other. So we go on vacations and leave the running of our companies to each other. But if one of us needs help, we are there in a flash. We are very supportive of each other. My mother still treats me as a youngster and I can honestly say I find it irritating. I try not to do the same to my daughter. I'm very proud of her."

"I don't really understand big family dynamics, as I don't have any. It sounds nice that you're all there for each other, even if you are not physically close."

"We do get into some family disputes, but mostly we are harmonious, because of our family rules."

"What are these rules?"

"We have positions in the family, like a corporation and we have to follow hierarchy if there is a dispute. We go to a higher family member to hear us out and they present a solution. This usually resolves all our problems, but sometimes resentment lasts a while. If it is too big a problem, it goes to the top and they have a council about the issue and create a mandate for family members to follow."

"Wow, your family must be powerful to go to all that trouble."

"Well, we live a long time so we have to get along with each other and this way has worked in my family for generations."

"You live a long time? Like a hundred?"

He laughs, "you will understand when you meet my family. It will make sense then."

"You say that like it's a sure thing. Have you decided I'm that important already?" I say as my hand grabs the side of the couch.

"Yes, I think so. Does that scare you?"

Taking a deep breath, "I think I'm behind you in my certainty. I want to know you and your family, but I'm still stuck on getting to know you right now."

"I love your honesty, Janan. Don't worry, take your time. We will go at your pace."

I take another breath, but this one is less stressful. I feel my muscles relaxing. A calmness is coming over me, along with the warm current from Eros's hand.

A warmth I want to feel more of. I want to feel him around me, holding me close, protecting me. *Wow*, I wonder, *that was the first time I ever felt that*. No man has ever made me feel like I want to be held for comfort or for protection. I can take care of myself, no need for a man to do that. I'm way too independent. But here is a great guy, and he respects my independence yet makes me want to lean on him. Or maybe my hormones just want him as close as I can get him. Or both.

Chapter 8

"Since I can't see you, I'd like to have some kind of idea about you physically. Would it be ok to feel your head and shoulders?" I ask with a shaky voice, wanting to feel more connected and also curious to see what he looks like.

"Sure. We can do that. Whatever helps you in this process."

He raises our hands and places my hands on his shoulders. They are broad and nicely muscled. He definitely works out, but not too much. Just a nice enough amount of muscle for definition. His body gives off an electric current in my hands. *Is this chemistry?* I wonder. I run my hands from his shoulders along the top to reach his neck and then I bring them up to his face. He has a clean-shaven face with a well-defined square jaw, just the way I like it. As I bring my hands higher on the sides of his face, I notice his short hair with a flair at the front. I bring my hands down to his nose and then down to his mouth. His lips are soft and I feel a sudden urge to kiss him. Slowly bringing myself closer, my hands go to the sides of his face. I hesitate, but he knows what I want and leans closer. I go for it and bring my mouth to his. Just like my hands, my lips feel his soft lips and current of electricity. The electricity tingles my lips and I feel the sensation move through my body, turning me on even more. He tastes like mint. He must have prepared just in case. His mouth kisses me softly, gently urging my mouth open. He uses his tongue and I melt. He puts his hands on the sides of my face, as my hands fall to his chest, feeling his muscles tighten. I love it when a man puts his hands around my face, makes me feel protected. His cologne engulfs me in its scent. He surrounds me, and I want to be even closer. We continue to devour each other as our hands wander. My hands run over his chest and then go around him, as I want to get as close as I can. One of his hands runs down my side then towards my lower back as he pulls me closer and then pulls me onto his lap. I moan as I straddle his legs and push myself onto him, feeling his desire against me. A rush of sexual energy courses through my body at the contact of him pressing against me. He releases a deep, satisfactory moan himself as I push against him harder. We continue to kiss deeply as my hands fall down his chest moving downwards until get to his belt. He breaks his kiss and reaches his hands to mine and pulls them away and back up to his chest.

"Not yet," he growls, "I want to, believe me, but we need to take our time."

Breathlessly, I answer, "But aren't I the one in control? I'd like to continue."

"That is such a turn on, but we really should go slow. I want you to be fully sure and I don't want to rush through this, and I don't want you to regret anything. I should leave now before you tempt me too much." He kisses me one more time but with only our lips and then he helps move me off of him and back onto the couch.

"I'll see you next week, Janan. Sleep well tonight if you can," he says, sounding like he was winking. He walks to the door and leaves.

I sit there on the couch, so turned on and disappointed and a little mad that he denied me. Yes, he was probably right, but damn I have needs too. I sigh in frustration and then head home. When I try to sleep, I keep having dreams that leave me sexually unsatisfied and that keeps me awake all weekend.

Chapter 9

The next Monday morning is definitely a coffee morning. Having hardly slept all weekend because of my sexual frustration, I shuffle to work. It takes me longer than usual to walk to work, but the cherry blossom trees help me feel better. Near work I grab a coffee and the warm sweetness from the sugar and cream make me slip out a moan on my first sip. Delicious heaven. I arrive at my desk a few minutes late, I'm the last one to arrive at work. We exchange greetings and then Max asks, "Why do you look so tired? Are you still seeing that guy every night? You're not doing anything reckless?"

"None of your business. My personal life is not up for conversation right now. I understand your concern, but I don't need a parent." I snap.

"Wow! So fierce. Where did that come from? You're too sweet to be talking like that."

"I'm no pushover, so mind your own business." I yank my chair back and drop into it.

Logging into my computer, I put some calming music on and then put on my headphones. Then I open my email account and see a message from Eros with his profile in it. I print it out to have a closer look at it on my break.

Later that day at lunch, I decide to sit by the waterfall by myself as I like to do from time to time when I need my own space. Today is not a day for dealing with people. Sighing out my exhaustion and frustration, I take a sip from my second coffee of the day. I am about to look at Eros' profile when Max appears beside me. "Hey, can I talk to you?" asks Max. Looking up, I say, "I'm not really in the mood to talk to you today."

"I know, and I'm sorry about what happened earlier. I worry, but to be honest, I'm jealous of the guy you're dating. It would be great to get to know you more. Can we go for dinner one night this week?".

"Oh...I didn't see that coming. I'm sorry, but I'm committed to getting to know the guy I'm dating. I don't have any free time anyway since I see him every weekday and my weekends are full of chores and seeing family."

"Oh ok. I guess I'm not good enough for you, am I?"

"That's not it at all," I reassure him. "I am just interested in this guy and want to see where it goes. It's nothing personal."

"Sure. I'll see you later." He leaves a bit hunched over with a frown on his forehead.

Max is unlike other men, as he didn't lose interest when he got to know me and saw my feisty side. That is something. But Eros is all I can think about. I don't like dating multiple people at the same time. It is too exhausting and hard to keep men separate as they start to overlap when you date more than one. But my friends have no problem doing it, saying you can't focus on one till you find the right match that becomes serious. Eros is weird but also considerate, funny, caring, confident, and such a good kisser.

I look at his profile now that I have a moment to do so. He is a CEO of a company that is unnamed. His age is forty-five, he is widowed, and he has a child. All things I already knew. Oh, he is learning Latin dancing. That's great, as I am learning as well. We could practice together. He is open to more children, which is nice, as I want one of my own. Also, he is into a healthy lifestyle, so he only drinks alcohol socially and doesn't smoke or do drugs. A goal of his is to find a partner to have a family with. His unusual skill is archery. This year, he wants to travel more. He knows English, Greek, French, Spanish, and Italian. Quite the polyglot! I wonder which language is his first and where he got that accent from. He wants to adopt a dog or cat. His favorite movie is City of Angels. And

CHAPTER 9

his favorite song is Queen's Bohemian Rhapsody. His profile is not unique. But it reaffirms what I've learned about him so far.

Thinking about his mouth speaking all those languages, makes me think of his lips. Oh, thinking of his kiss would not help me now. I need to focus on work today. Standing up to go back to work, I smile to myself, thinking, *tonight should be enjoyable.*

Sitting on the couch waiting for Eros in my green spring dress with white flowers that I'm wearing tonight on purpose; unable to sit still in anticipation, I think of him. He is a man you take notice of for sure. No wonder he said I will know him once I see him. I can't wait to see him. But it seems so far away, there is still a little less than one week to go. What if I'm wrong about him? I don't want to get caught up in these emotions. I need to be careful. But I'm so attracted to him even though I haven't seen him.

After what feels like an eternity, the front door opens. "Hi Janan, I brought you a surprise." Eros calls out.

"Oh, what is it?"

"Here" Eros stops at the end of the couch beside me. He reaches out his hand to find my shoulder. "Place your hands in front of you," he directs. I do so and feel a bouquet of flowers. I bring them to my nose, "Oh lilacs! They smell amazing." I smell them for a little longer and then place them on the table. "I'll put them in a vase when I get home. Their calming smell will help me sleep."

As Eros sits down beside me, he asks, "So, you had trouble sleeping this weekend as well?" laughing he continues, "I did too."

"Yes! And then I had to deal with my coworker at work today. No peace. But I look forward to tonight."

"What do you mean you had to deal with a coworker?" He says tightly.

"Oh well, one of my coworkers was getting on my case about dating you and then he asked me out. I turned him down, but today was very frustrating."

"He's not allowed to do that during company hours. Who is he?" How does he know what our company rules are? Why is he so angry that Max asked me out at work?

"Well, it was on our lunch break. But I dealt with it. He seems overly grouchy to me, since he's upset about me dating you."

"I don't like him bothering you at work."

"Thank you for your concern, but I dealt with it. I was very clear."

"I love that about you. Your frankness and protecting your boundaries."

"Oh, thanks. That's not how men usually see me and when they do, they usually leave."

"That's because they are not real men. They want a woman who can't take care of themselves just for their ego."

"I've never thought of it that way. It's a fascinating concept. I like it." I feel the electricity even though we aren't touching. His reaction turns me on. No man has seen me as well as Eros.

Eros leans closer and puts his hands on my shoulders, turning me towards him fully. "Thank you for honoring our agreement. It means so much to me that you are taking this seriously. And I don't like other men hitting on you, especially at work. I trust you, but I still don't like it." He puts a hand on the side of my face and puts his lips on mine. It is a slow, tender kiss. I feel the electricity intensify. My body yearns for his touch. I want more. He pulls away. "How come you're not wearing sleeves? Aren't you cold?" then rubs his hands down my arms.

"I'm not cold. I wanted to wear a spring dress today. The day called for it. It was so nice out today."

He laughs. "A dress! Are you trying to tempt me? The things I could do to you." *Yes, that was the point of wearing this dress today.*

"Oh, please do"

He grabs me and hugs me tightly. "We are going to take our time. I told you before I don't want you to regret anything. We have all the time in the world. There's no need to rush." His hug is comforting and arousing at the same time. I want him completely.

CHAPTER 9

"Have you ever thought that maybe I have needs that need tending to?"

"Oh, then I must take care of your needs, but I will only kiss you today."

He continues to kiss me slowly and tenderly, making me slowly fill up with warm energy. Then he pulls me up onto the couch and lies on top of me. He kisses my neck, tickling me into pleasure. I reach for his shoulders and back, feeling his muscles. *Wow, he's built nicely.* I push up against him, wanting to feel him. One of his hands goes down my leg and pulls my dress up. Reaching for my underwear, "You're not wearing underwear either. Oh, the big guns are out today, I see. Well, I won't disappoint you." He presses his thumb against me, making me eager for more. The electricity from his thumb makes me feel even more sensitive and aroused. As he plays with my clitoris with one hand, his other hand goes to lift my dress higher up. He then goes lower and uses his mouth, kissing me as he promised. Electricity and the movement of his tongue brings me higher in arousal, faster than I've ever experienced before. Swirls of ecstasy begin inside of me. I begin to climb in pleasure, wanting more. As Eros works on my clitoris with his tongue, licking and sucking me, I feel truly desired. It is an important feeling that I hadn't really felt before. The thought makes me more in tune with Eros and what he is doing to me. It makes it feel more special. And it makes me warm up even more. After a while of Eros playing with me and me telling him what I like, waves of ecstasy roll through my body as I come. I hold his head, not wanting to lose my high. As I come back down to reality, he gets up to lie beside me on the couch, closely holding onto me.

"Now it's your turn," I sigh in pleasure.

"No, today was just for you. I can wait."

"Why are you doing this for real Eros? Why this blind dating?"

"As I've said before, I want a genuine connection. Not one that's based on superficial things. I want a woman who wants me for me, not for things I have."

"Yes, but you've told me that women want you for that. Aren't you worried I'd just want the same since you said it?"

"No, as I'm getting to know you, I'm finding that I'm not worried about you. I've learned you are a woman who takes care of herself and you don't depend on others for superficial things. You go after what you want on your own."

"Yes, I believe we share our lives with our partners and we should support each other, not just demand things from one another."

"I agree. I hope you are getting to know me as well. What have you learned about me?"

"You are kind and see to my needs. You are ambitious and take pride in your work. But, more importantly, you are caring and loving with your family and friends and express your love with time spent together and providing food. Your strong will keeps you from losing control. I would like to see how much control you can keep if I keep seducing you, but I respect your boundaries, so I won't do that tonight."

Talking late into the night, we each head home separatelyl. This might work out. High from my orgasm, I float home, hopeful for the future.

Chapter 10

The next day at work is tense, as Max hunches over his desk, ignoring everyone and mumbling to himself once in a while.

"Do you know what happened to him?" whispers Anne.

"Let's just leave him alone. He'll get over it," I whisper back. I didn't want to get into it. I didn't want to embarrass him, but I also didn't want a lecture from the others as well for dating Eros.

We work in silence throughout the day. Wanting some space, I go to eat my lunch outside at my usual place. Anne comes over and sits beside me. "I know something happened between you and Max. He keeps looking at you and then mutters to himself."

"Oh well, he doesn't agree with my dating choices, is all."

"Well, it's obvious he likes you. He usually tries to save the seat next to him for you at lunch."

"Oh well, I turned him down yesterday. Please don't tell anyone."

"I won't. But we are all worried about this guy you're dating."

I turn toward her and smile, saying, "It's weird, but it's going really well. Sure, I don't know what he looks like, but he talks about himself openly. I feel like I know him better than any other man I've dated."

She smiles sadly. "That sounds great, but I'm still worried that he's lying to you. Is there a way you can check if he's being honest about himself?"

My back becomes tense as I reply, "Not any more than I could check other guys I could date. Sure, maybe if I knew his name I could research him, but that's not something I do. Plus, he sent me his dating profile, and it matches what he says about himself."

"Oh," she says, sitting up straighter, "I guess that's true. That's great that he sent you his profile. We just worry about you. Be careful ok?"

"I am being careful. I listen to what he says. He doesn't contradict himself and he sounds very genuine when he talks. I trust him."

"That's all good, but until you know who he is, I wouldn't trust him. I just want you to be safe."

Relaxing my posture, I reply, "Thanks for your concern, but I got this. I promise I will think more about what you said. Let's get back."

After work, I have some time to kill before I meet with Eros. In the break room, I call Chloe to catch her up on things.

"Hey Hey, how's it going sis?" She answers her phone.

"It's going great. Work is going well, besides this guy who hit on me and is now upset about it. My coworkers are worried for me about Eros, even though he's such a great guy. I feel like Eros and I are clicking as we get to know each other more."

"How close are you getting?"

"Close," I say, looking down at the ground.

"Hmm. Well, what do you know about this guy? How do you know if he's being honest?"

Squeezing my phone "The same amount I would know about any other guy I could date. You don't know, you just have to trust the process and pay attention

CHAPTER 10

to what they say and see what they do to see if they are being honest." I stand up and walk around the table in slow circles.

"Ok calm down, I get it. Just please take your time getting to know him before you get too close. I just worry about you."

"Well, I'm going with the flow and I'm enjoying myself. There's no reason not to. He is not like the other guys I date. He likes me and appreciates my personality, and doesn't pull away when I ask him questions, and he likes my confidence."

"That's awesome. I'm glad you found someone who can value you. He sounds like a great guy. I hope it all works out. It's just this weird situation that makes me uneasy, so please be careful."

"I get your uneasiness. I have been listening closely to what he says."

As I hang up the phone with Chloe, I slump back into my chair in the break room. Am I being careful enough? Am I seeing him through rose-colored glasses? But as far as I could tell, he is being genuine. What if he is lying? What would he be lying about? We don't talk about work, so I don't know if his saying he's a CEO is true. We both go home every night separately, so he could be going back to his wife. But he doesn't wear a ring. Unless he takes it off when he goes to the condo. But he said he's been married before, but he's single now. The everyday life stuff isn't extravagant, so there's no need to lie there. What he does when he's not at the condo with me, might be what I need to learn about him. To know if he's telling the truth is impossible, but I can see if he contradicts himself. I don't want to distrust him, but I need to look out for myself.

Sitting on my hands, I feel goosebumps on my arms. I'm unable to sit still. Moving from side to side, I try to relax. I don't know how today will go, but I must try to see if he's lying about anything. He seems so great and accepting of me. That is huge to me. I like him a lot already, I can tell. Wanting to be right about him and wanting to trust him, I worry as other people seem so worried about this way of dating, but it's not really that different from real dating. I just can't see him, that's all. I don't know his real name either...that's more of a concern to me. But he said he'd reveal himself after a month. But will he? Or will he just disappear? Oh, I don't like this uneasiness. I just want to enjoy the moment with him. Can't I? Do I have to worry? Agh.

"Janan?" I jump in my seat. Oh crap, I didn't hear him.

"Hi Eros, I'm in my usual place."

"I'll come sit by you if that's ok?"

"Sure" I want to feel him. "Can we hug hello?'

"Definitely," He gives me a soft squeeze. "Did you sleep ok last night?"

"I did. It was a good sleep." I laugh and pull him close for another hug. "Did you sleep ok?"

"No, I kept thinking of you last night. But I got to sleep in today,as I had a day off." He kept his hold on me.

"Oh, a day off, lucky!" I push him back a bit and take his head into my hands and kiss him softly and slowly. Then I use my tongue, urging his mouth to open. He does and then we kiss each other deeply. I suck his tongue and he moans. He pulls back saying "We just got here, let's talk first."

"We can talk later. I want you now." Pulling him towards me for more, I know I want him, not even caring if he's lying or not. I want to trust him. He feels so right. So warm and so much energy comes off of him, it makes my skin tingle. I pull back. "Let's go to the bedroom."

"We shouldn't. We need to keep calm and take our time. Oh, Janan, I want you but we need to go slow. You need to know me before we have sex."

This statement makes me want Eros even more. He must not be lying. Does he want to wait till I know him? No man would wait that long. I can't wait that long. "Thank you for your consideration, but I don't want to wait."

"I love your frankness and I understand your needs, but I cannot go further right now."

"Then please me like you did yesterday and hold me close."

"I will hold you, but nothing more today. I don't think I'd be able to stop myself if we do anything more." He pulls me to my feet and we walk close to the

CHAPTER 10

wall, where we can feel our way to the bedroom. We reach the bed and he lays down beside me and brings me to him so that I am laying at his side with my arm and leg on him. "Let's talk and hold each other. But no more kissing," he says.

Sighing, I reply "Well, if we are just talking, tell me about what you like to do outside of work hours?"

"Well, besides my hobbies that I told you about and seeing family and friends, I like to go people-watching. I go to a cafe or another busy place and make up stories about the different people I see and sometimes if it's people I've seen before and know a little about them from watching and listening to them, I push them into the path of their crush so they can start a new love story."

"Like an actual god of love. Making people come together."

"You can join me next time. Sometimes it's boring, but when you see signs of crushes, it's hard not to meddle. You help make a happy ever after for people."

"You should work for my company. You'd fit right in. Maybe work in the coaching department."

"Maybe, but the job I have is fun as well. I quite enjoy it. When you know my job you will think I'm well suited to it as well."

"Oh, a mystery. I have to wait to find out. I can't wait to know. Can you tell me more about your past relationships?"

"Sure. I've dated but have only found one love who I married a long time ago. As I mentioned before, she was special and saw me for who I was and we were married until her passing. It was really hard for a while after she died. I loved her so much. We were very happy. I hope to find this same love with you. I think you are special too. You have potential."

"I'm sorry to hear you had a hard time. You must have loved her a lot. You must have been really young when you married." *How old was Eros?* His profile says he is forty-five. Well, that's not too old. Ten years' difference is ok with me.

"A lot younger than now, yes. We should get going, it's getting late," he rumbles beside me.

"Can we just stay here tonight? I'm comfortable and don't want to move. I want to stay longer with you."

"You mean you want to spend the whole night here?"

"Yes."

"I have to get up early, but otherwise I can stay most of the night with you."

Phew, he must not have someone at home if he can stay. It makes me happy that he's willing to stay. Even though he won't be physical with me.

"Then let's stay here tonight. I want to cuddle with you more."

As we lay there cuddling, my eyes close. It is getting harder and harder to keep them open. As I drift off to sleep, he kisses my forehead.

Chapter 11

I wake up slowly, feeling Eros beside me. My neck feels cramped from leaning on Eros' shoulder. I can't see him. The blackout curtains keep all the light out. I listen and hear him sleeping, breathing softly. I realize I still have my phone in my pocket. A thought comes over me. I could do it and he wouldn't notice. It is so tempting, but the plan is to see him face to face next week. I could wait for that, right? I should believe him and wait, but I could also sneak a peek…What if he's lying about seeing me and disappears? How would I know who he was then? How would I find him again, if I didn't know who he was, and he leaves? But he's been so open about who he is and he's been so great to get to know. I could trust him, couldn't I? He is a great catch and I believe he will show himself to me. But what if he's not who he says he is? What if he is really old? He never told me directly how old he was, just that he looked around thirty and his profile age could be a lie. What if he was involved with illegal work? What if knowing who he is makes me an accomplice? My curiosity wins. I need to see him.

I slide my phone out of my pocket slowly. I bring it up to my head. I feel for the button on the side to turn the screen on. I listen for Eros again, still breathing softly. I push the button with a soft click. Light comes on and shows Eros sleeping beside me. His hair is a dark blond color, styled in a quiff with spikes. He has a chiseled jaw, making me want to bite it. His nose is straight and large, but not overly large, it fits his face well. His lips look delicious and pink. I want to kiss them. He has broad shoulders and there are golden feathers behind his shoulders that flashes in the light of my phone. Wait what? He has wings? His breathing stops. I look at his face and see his eyes are blue and sparkling....wait oh shit.

"What are you doing?! You broke your promise to me." He says, pushing me off of him.

He is Daniel Lennon, CEO of Matchmaker. My boss!

"What are you doing? Turn the light off! It's dangerous to see me unprepared." He says, sitting up in bed. "I can't believe you! I thought you were trustworthy. I thought you trusted me." He yells.

"I, I'm sorry, but I had to know. You know who I am. You're my boss! Isn't this illegal? Hiding who you are?"

"Won't you turn the light off? Why do women never trust me? Why do you all have to be so curious? I thought you'd be different. We're done." He says, standing up. His wings seemed to have disappeared. Did I imagine them?

"Daniel, please don't go, I'm sorry."

"I told you to call me Eros but I guess Daniel is all you'll get."

"What does that mean? You're confusing me." My voice shakes from shock.

"Goodbye Janan." He walks out of the room.

"Wait" I yell after him.

I hear the front door slam shut. He is gone.

What have I done? He just left with little effort. He didn't even try to talk about it. Did I mean so little that it was over from just one second of making a wrong choice? Did that mean I was just a fling? He was so final in his voice and words. I can fix this. This was just a mistake. Right? I know I broke his trust in me, but he just walked away. Is he worth the effort? I need to talk to him to see if he is the man I think he is and fix our relationship or see if I should end it.

Chapter 12

I sped to the office, almost losing a shoe, as I didn't put them on quite right in my rush to talk to Daniel. I just got in the elevator as it closed. Luckily, no one else was in it. It was early to be at work, but I felt Daniel would be in his office. Honestly, I did not know where else he could be. Hoping he'd be in, I couldn't stop shaking and breathing in and out as I counted to five. I need to calm down. He was angry because I didn't trust him enough. I understood I broke his trust, but he also wasn't honest enough. He said he knew me, but being my boss was unethical, wasn't it? I am at a disadvantage, I barely know him, but he has all the information about me. Not only was I an employee, but I was also in Matchmaker's database, as I signed up for the dating service.

Leaning against the metal wall, feeling its coolness. I am shaking and squeezing my hands into fists. Wanting to make things right, I also need him to understand that abandoning me that quickly and not even talking it out was unacceptable. It brought up emotions that were hard to control. A deep sense that I was going to be left behind again. Falling in love is scary. You have to trust the person would always be there for you and you couldn't control that. People leave our lives all the time. My parents, for example, left this world suddenly. My sister and I were orphans in an instant. No way to bring them back. We had to learn to live without them. I didn't want that for my future love life, so I protect myself from falling in love. But still Eros made me fall hard. I didn't want to be without him. It's hard for me to trust men, as they tend to just leave me as I start to like them. They find my setting boundaries unappealing. Eros was different. He appreciates them. He made me hope for a future where I could trust in love and a man who would not leave me. But then he leaves me! I don't know where to go from here. But, I think I need to talk to him. Maybe we could work this out. I want this to work out.

I remember seeing gold wings behind him. That wasn't real, was it? Was I still half asleep? And what did he mean by "Daniel is all you'll get?"

The door pings, and I am finally at Daniel's office. The doors open and the posh secretary in a black pants suit with dirty blond hair in a ponytail picks up the phone and says, "she's here." Out walks a tall, confident, and stunning blond woman dressed to kill in her floral blazer, black blouse, and jeans. She has a necklace with a giant pearl that fancies up her outfit. "Well, you have more gumption than I thought with you coming here," she says as she places her left hand on her hip. Impatiently waiting for my response.

"Umm hi, I'm here to see Daniel. Is he in?" I breathe out.

"He told you to call him by a different name, didn't he? Be careful which name you use. It could decide more than you think." She shot out.

"I don't understand, but is Eros here, then?"

"Yes, use the name he gave you. No, he's not in. You'll have to deal with me."

"And who are you?" Scared of the answer, I shift my feet.

"Well, that's a good question. You can call me Zoe for now. We'll see if you get my real name. I'm disappointed in you. You were so close to learning everything about Eros. You only had a week left. Such a shame. He's very selective about who gets to know him. I don't think I'll help you." That's good. Then she's not his wife. But how will I find Eros?

"Please tell me where I can find him. We just need to talk it out."

"Maybe. Tell me," she says hesitantly, "Is there anything you noticed about him that shows you how special he is?"

"He's so caring and considerate," I start.

CHAPTER 12

"Not that stuff, but it's good to know that about him. I mean, anything really different?"

"He always makes me feel alive when we are together. And maybe...but I think I was hallucinating"

"Maybe what? This is important."

"He had gold wings for a minute," I whisper.

"Are you sure they were gold or were they white?"

"Definitely gold. Does this mean anything to you? And...well you have a giant pearl necklace. I didn't know pearls were that big."

"The potential you have is rare. You really fucked up. But gold is a very important color. And the pearl you see is unexpected, many cannot see it. It's an old piece that goes back to my birth, but that's another story. I'll help you a little, but it will come at a cost."

"So I'm not hallucinating? Am I really seeing these things? Thank you for helping me. I need to talk to him. What do I need to do?"

"Don't thank me yet. I will be putting you to the test. This will not be easy."

"I will do whatever I need to do to see him again."

Chapter 13

"It so happens Matchmaker is having a special private event tonight. It is for our premium members. We need help to get ready. After work, you'll need to go down to the event room and sort all the profile packages for the attendees at the speed dating event tonight." Zoe dictates.

"But I work in marketing research, which doesn't seem to be related to my job," I respond.

"Look, do you want my help or not? You will do the tasks I assign or you can forget about Eros."

"I'll do it. But how will this help me get to Eros?"

"By my good graces, I will tell you where you can find him if you do all the tasks I ask of you. You need to learn about our business in all areas to be a suitable partner for Eros. You need to know how to do the minor jobs, so you can be a good leader for the company."

"Oh, thank you. I will get to work then," feeling relieved, I smile at Zoe.

"Let's see how you do first," she warns.

After work, I take the elevator down to the first floor and walk into the event room. I was feeling hopeful as I went there. Zoe didn't seem that bad; she is willing to help me. But I wonder what she means to Daniel, no Eros. I don't know why the name I use matters, but I will be careful to use the name he gave me. Maybe it means I was close to him, like a family nickname or something. I feel lightheaded and I can't focus. Why do I have to earn Zoe's trust? It was Eros' trust I lost. But I want to be with Eros again, so I will earn both of their trust, if that's what it takes to get him back.

The room is large and there is a table covered in boxes. I guess that's where I would find the profile packages. When I get to the table, there are so many boxes piled up. The boxes have different papers in each of them. I take one page out of each box and find the order of pages for the packages. When I look at the pages, I notice that the theme for the event was based on Greek Mythology. And the names of the people signed up for the packages all have Greek names, like Hermes, Poseidon, and Dionysus. Why is Eros so obsessed with Greek mythology? I shrug and start sorting the boxes so that they are more orderly, this way I can easily go from one box to the next to create the packages. I leave the tables free so I can put out the profile packages on them. While sorting the boxes helped, it was clear I cannot finish all of it myself. Sighing, I put on some music and got to work.

"Here you are. Why are you still here after hours?" asks Max.

I jump at his voice. I am so occupied by my work and the music, I didn't hear him come in. "Oh, you scared me, Max."

"Sorry, I didn't realize how engrossed you were. What are you doing here? This work isn't part of our job descriptions?"

"Oh, I volunteered to help out."

"Did you? That seems weird. We have enough work as it is." "That's true. I just want to do it."

CHAPTER 13

"Ok. You look like you have a good system going. But there's too much work here for just one person. Is anyone helping you?"

"No, it's just me. Honestly, I don't think I'll finish in time, so I need to get back to it."

"I'm done with my work for the day. I'll help."

"Oh, you don't have to."

"I know, but this is definitely a multi-person job. I don't mind."

"Ok, thanks," I say with a bit of relief. I don't want to fail this task. We get to work. Chatting as we file the profile packages and neatly place them on the table for the event. With Max's help, we finish with thirty minutes to spare.

"Thank you so much for your help. I would never have this done in time." I say as I hug him.

"No problem! Let's go for a drink to celebrate finishing."

"Oh, I can't. I have to report back to the volunteer lead. Sorry, rain check?"

"Sure. Don't forget," he says, winking at me.

"I won't. I owe you a drink. Thanks so much for helping me out!"

"Anytime, I'm always here to help you," he says warmly.

I sigh inside, not wanting to hurt him but being clear I'm not interested I say "Thanks Max, you're a great friend. Let me know if you ever need help, too." Yes, I played the friend card. It's clear enough on its own. At least I hope so. "I gotta get going. See you tomorrow."

I take the elevator up to the top floor to Eros's office. The secretary calls Zoe and then lets me into the office. The office has a sleek metal desk with a glass top at the back of the room with a stylish black chair to sit in. In front of the desk are some gray couches facing each other and a big gray chair at the top right in front of the desk between the couches. It reminds me of an office you'd find in a Korean drama. There are bookshelves behind the desk full of books and nicknacks. Zoe was standing by the couches and waves me over. I sit on the couch nearby and she sits in the head chair, the place of power. She was making sure I knew who was in charge.

"So, how did you manage to get it all done on time? Please tell me your secrets," Zoe asks.

"Well, honestly, I had a friend stop by and help me."

"You asked your friends to help you? It was a task for only you for a reason," she says sternly.

"I didn't ask. He just showed up on his own. I did the task either way."

"Yes, you did. Tomorrow, you will help again after work. I'll send you the information tomorrow. For now, go home and rest."

"I have to meet Eros at the condo." I hope he will show up.

"Don't bother, he won't be there. Just go home and rest. If you do well, you'll see him soon enough."

"Well, this isn't just about him, you know. I am angry too." I sputter, "He just abandoned me. He didn't even try to talk things out."

"Yes, that's true, but there is more to Eros than you know. He gets hurt by female curiosity all the time. None of the women he dates ever trust him fully. He thought you were different, that you trusted him enough. You have potential and that is the only reason I am helping you. But you have to earn my help. Go home and rest. In time, you will see him again and talk about your problems together." She says in a kinder voice than before.

I leave feeling defeated. My feet drag on the way home. I go straight to bed feeling like I have a mountain to climb tomorrow.

Chapter 14

The next day was a slog at work. I barely slept and work is getting busy with the new promotions. I thought about Eros all night. But at work, I am too busy to think about anything else, which is a slight relief. Getting fixated on my problems wouldn't help any, only make my day worse. Wondering if this or that wouldn't fix anything either. We need to talk to each other, but in order to do that, I need to do the tasks Zoe instructs me to do. They would be a grand gesture of my effort to work things out. Hopefully, Eros will see that and have an open discussion with me.

My growling stomach reminds me it is lunchtime. The day is flying past me. I turn to my coworkers, "Hey guys, ready for lunch?"

"Oh yes, just give me five minutes to finish this section," replies Philip.

"Same here," says Anne.

"I'm ready to go," says Max.

"Great. Max and I will go down and grab a table for all of us. Come when you're ready."

We walk to the elevator and take it down to the cafeteria. Sitting at the table, Max looks serious for a moment, studying me. "Everything ok?" he asks.

"Yes, just tired from volunteering yesterday. Thanks for your help again."

"I thought you were visiting with that guy and now you are volunteering for extra work at work," he pushes.

"Well, sometimes you need to go the extra mile to be noticed." I evade.

Just then, the others come to the table. Max doesn't push any further with the others there. We chat and eat our lunches. It feels more like a normal day of work, which is a relief.

After lunch, the day flies past me as well. Suddenly, it's four o'clock, and my email dings with a new message from Zoe. She has my next task ready. Reading the email, I sigh as I hate the next task. It is more in line with promotion, but it is on the ground marketing of handing out fliers. I enjoy doing marketing but not handing out fliers. People never want them and you feel like a nuisance. But this would help me get to Eros.

"How do you know Zoe Lennon? And why is she asking you to do fliers?" Asks Anne, who is just behind me..

"Oh! You shouldn't be reading over my shoulder." I retort.

"I didn't mean to, but that's from Zoe. How do you know her? It's so hard to get to know upper management."

"I ran into her the other day and she is helping me reach a goal of mine."

"Is that why you were volunteering yesterday? Because of Zoe?" asks Max.

"You guys are way too nosey."

"Are you trying to get into upper management? That's a big difference from marketing research." asks Phillip.

"No, I'm not, but there is a goal thatI'm after."

"So hush-hush with yourself lately. We are just looking out for you." Anne says with a hurt voice.

"I appreciate it, but there are some things I can't share at work."

"You are handing out fliers tonight. Do you want help?" Anne says, ignoring me.

"I'm supposed to do these tasks alone apparently to help build my skill set? But thanks for offering."

"Why do you have to do them alone? That makes little sense," Phillip says.

"It's like a private mentorship, I guess."

CHAPTER 14

"Ok. But make sure it's still fair. Don't overwork yourself either." Anne says.

"Thanks, guys. Sorry for being sensitive about it. But it's something I decided to do so I will do my best."

"You have a lot of sensitive stuff going on. If you need anything, please let us know. We worry about you." Anne reassures me.

"Thanks. I'm going to head out to get ready. See you tomorrow."

Reaching Waterfront Station, the location for the flier distribution, there is a table set up with boxes of fliers. Well, this will be fun. There are so many fliers here. Do I have to give out all of them? A woman approaches me. She has short amber pixie hair and wears a black cropped blouse with jeans and black low heels. She looks normal enough, except she has elf ears. I didn't know that pointy ears were real.

"Hi! You must be Janan. I'm Becca. I'm here to help you get started. Your goal today is to hand out all these fliers. It's best to keep them in their boxes so they don't fly away. You can grab a handful at a time so you don't strain yourself. Just a tip. Women are more supportive of our fliers, but we need more men to join. So please try to hand fliers out to the men as well. If you have a musical voice, it seems to get people's attention and it will be easier for you to hand out the fliers. You can start when you're ready. I suggest trying a few different catchphrases to see what gets attention. The one that we have that's the most well-received is: 'Are you fed up with dating apps? Try Matchmaker, get your first match free with this coupon!'"

"Wow, thanks for the orientation, Becca. Will you be staying around?"

"No. But I'll be back at seven to see how you're doing."

"Ok, thanks. See you later." I look at the boxes and see hundreds of fliers. This will take a lot of time. Well, I'd better get started.

I pick up a stack of fliers and get to work. Using the slogan that Becca gave me, the fliers lessen. I try changing my voice to sound more appealing and smooth as well, since Becca said that would help. Going back to the table for more every twenty minutes, the fliers seem to be popular and are disappearing quickly. And women definitely are more open to taking them. But men seem to respond to the voice I found that sounds like a mezzo-soprano. But it seems weird that the fliers were disappearing so fast. As I go back out into the station handing out fliers, I keep an eye out for the table of fliers. That's when I see it. Max sneaking over to the table and grabbing a stack of fliers, and rushing away to the other side of the station. What the hell! I'm supposed to do this on my own. Zoe won't let me see Eros again if I get help from others. Ugh! Why can't people let me be? I told all of them I need to do this alone. So why is he here?

Fuming, I walk over to Max. No way is he going to ruin my chance of seeing Eros again. I found him by the restaurant handing out fliers. I walk right up to him and grab the fliers out of his hands. "What are you doing? Are you trying to ruin my chances of reaching my goal? I told you I had to do this alone."

"There's no way you could do all those fliers by yourself. It's not fair of them to ask you to do it."

"That's none of your business. You need to stop and go home. Don't help me anymore because your help will make me lose him!" I blurt out by accident.

"Lose who? The guy you're dating? Good! He's not good enough for you, acting all weird about dating you. Was that your goal? What does Zoe have to do with the guy you're dating?"

"It doesn't matter. It's my business and I don't want your help. Please stop helping and let me do what I have to do."

"Fine. I know when I'm not wanted, but you should give up on that guy. He doesn't sound like a good guy. You deserve someone who appreciates you. Not some weird situation where you date in secret, without seeing him, and then do tasks for other people just to see him again. It makes no sense!"

"I know what it sounds like, but it's my life and I need to do what I feel is necessary for me. And that is finishing this task *alone*." I storm off back to my area of the station and continue to hand out fliers. The fliers are harder to sell since I am in a darker mood than earlier. I try to forget the argument and focus on my task, but it is hard. Max has a point. But I have a goal to see Eros again.

CHAPTER 14

I pass the rest of the time giving out flier after flier until I am exhausted. I go back to the table and notice it's after seven and Becca has returned. She's holding the last box. Walking over and feeling like I lost as I didn't finish in time.

"Hey, guess what? You did it! The boxes are all empty. How did you do it?" Becca beams.

"I did! That's awesome!" But then I remember I had help, "but I didn't do all of it. Someone from work stopped by and helped me out without my knowledge. I stopped him, but that means I didn't do it all on my own."

"Janan, I watched you and you were awesome. I saw your passion for Matchmaker. I also saw your friend and your fight. Don't worry, you didn't know. You dealt with it. I will tell Zoe all about it." Becca reassures me. "Go home and rest. You did a great job today."

"Thanks, Becca." I walk home from the station. It takes about thirty minutes, but it is a nice evening out. I think again about Max. He has some excellent points, and he keeps helping me out. He's not a bad guy, but he just doesn't understand that I don't need his help. I'm not a lost little lamb needing guidance. I'm a woman on a mission. He would make a great boyfriend for a girl who relies on her man a lot. But that's not me. When I need help, I ask for it, but I can do things on my own. I don't need a nanny to take care of all the little things for me. It's suffocating. But he wouldn't just abandon me like Eros. Here he is helping me even though I've already told him I'm not interested several times. And even though it's against my wishes, he is still trying to make me happy. Reaching home, I fall into bed and sleep through the night for the first time in days.

Chapter 15

I wake up feeling refreshed. I am ready to take on the day. The cherry blossoms are still in full bloom and walking past them lifts my spirit. Nature always reminds you of life and how precious it is. Arriving at work, I'm a little tense as I am worried how Max will act towards me. He is a good guy, but I seem to keep hurting him. I don't want to seem ungrateful for his help, but I don't want to encourage him, either.

"Good morning dear! You look much better today. You have your energy back. Did you get back together with that blind date guy?" Anne asks.

"No, not yet. But I slept well last night. Was I making you worry? Sorry about that. Just been doing some extra work the past few days."

"Yes, I hope management takes notice of your volunteering. What position are you trying to apply for?" Phillip asks.

"Oh, I'm not trying to apply for another job. I'm just trying to do some good deeds for my own selfish reasons." I wish I could say it wasn't pro bono, but rather it's to see Eros again. I hope that doesn't make me too selfish.

"Well, good luck with it either way. What are you helping with today?" Phillip asks.

"Thanks. I'm not sure yet. Still waiting to hear. But we got some important work to do today to prepare for the end of the quarter, so hopefully nothing will happen till the end of the day."

"Oh yes, we do. Thanks for the reminder. Hopefully, Max will be here shortly, so we can get on it."

"Did someone just say my name? What timing! Yes, let's get to it," Max says, sliding into his seat.

It is good to see Max being normal at work. I'm glad he wasn't upset about our argument last night. We start our meeting by mapping out our tasks for the day so that we can finish our project that was due soon. Which is the project to find what was causing problems for clients while they were using our online services and it was progressing well. We have narrowed down the potential problems to the top five that need immediate attention and have found solutions to fix them. We just need to prepare the presentation for the digital team that would have to do the work of fixing the problems. The day goes by quickly, as we all work hard on our tasks. I am so focused on work I skip lunch, only eating some snacks I store at my desk. I am in a flow state and suddenly; it is the end of the day. We are close to finishing the end of the quarter project, with only a few final touches left.

I am getting ready to keep on working once everyone leaves, but I get an email from Zoe. There are instructions to go pick up a package for Zoe and bring it to her. I don't understand how this job is linked to Matchmaker, as my previous tasks had been. I check the address, and it is for a large makeup company called Sephora on Robson Street. Not that far a walk. It should only take thirty minutes. I could do the task and still have time to do the final touches on my team's project.

I walk with a quick step to get back to work as soon as I can. I reach the store in no time. Finding an employee of the store, I ask for help. She leads me to the back desk and hands me over to the woman there. "Hi, I'm here to pick up a package for Zoe Lennon." I start, but she cuts me off, "Sorry we do not have any package for that name."

"Well, she sent me over here to pick it up. Could you check one more time?"

"There is nothing here for that name," she insists.

"Oh I see, I'll go ask her. Maybe she got the location wrong." I walk away, annoyed at the worker. Oh course, this is the location. Why couldn't they find the order? I'd have to ask Zoe for help. Walking towards the door, a young woman in a green blouse with jeans and white sneakers. She has bright rainbow hair in a swept-back long pixie style and blue eyeshadow to kill for, brushing past me, and whispers, "Think harder. You'll get it."

I stop in my tracks. What did she mean? Think about what? Why did Zoe send me here when there was nothing for her? This was a test? What am I missing? She said to call her Zoe for now...that means like Eros, maybe she has another name. What could it be? Who is closely associated with Eros in Greek mythology? The only name I could think of was Aphrodite. The goddess of love. Was Zoe Daniel's mother? Was this name thing a weird family game?

Turning around, I go back to the desk. The employee looks up and sighs. I smile and ask, "Would you have something for Aphrodite?"

"Oh, you're here for the special package, sure let me get that for you." She goes through the back door and comes out with a fancy golden rectangular box. "Here you go. Please sign here that you picked it up," I sign and leave the store triumphantly with the box. I don't see the woman who helped me. She seems to have disappeared.

Walking back to work, I wonder why Zoe went by Aphrodite and Daniel by Eros. Were they huge Ancient Greek fans? Was it because of their matchmaking business? Also, what was in this box? Makeup I guess? But the box was not a typical box you would get at a makeup store. It's made of a light wood painted in gold. There is nothing locking the box. I could take a peek and see what Zoe got, and no one would know. It's very tempting to get to know Zoe more.

I look at the box. It was a test. I shouldn't have been able to pick up the box in the first place, as Zoe didn't give me the name it was under. And it looks like it was probably only makeup, nothing I need to see. Plus, didn't Eros yell at me that women were too curious for their own good? And this definitely is a test. Hmm. I think I'll be cautious and not look. Walking back to work, I enjoy the fresh air as I wonder more about Eros and Zoe, or should I say, Aphrodite.

Reaching work, I go up the elevator to Eros' office to give Zoe the box. She is waiting for me at the secretary's desk. "How did you get that box? How did you get Persephone to give it to you? Why are you here? Did you not open it?" She demands.

"I have my secret ways of doing things," I retort, "here's your box." Who was Persephone? Another ancient Greek fan? Were there a bunch of them? Was there a community of people who go by gods' and goddesses' names?

"Don't you wonder what's inside?"

"Sure, but it's not mine to look at."

"That speaks very well for you. It shows that we can trust you. You have great potential. But there is one test left. Please open the box and tell me what you see."

I take back the box, wondering what I need to see inside. I open it and some purple mist comes out of the box. It makes me tired. Trying to focus on what was in the box, I see what's inside. "A golden arrow," I say as I fall to the floor.

Chapter 16

"She lasted long enough to see what was inside the box and she saw your golden wings. She has more potential than you know. This one might make it." I hear Zoe say as I begin to wake up. I don't get what's going on, but I am tired of being tested. Was a guy really worth all this trouble? Even a guy who made me feel so connected. He was worth it, I think. At least until he left me behind.

"I know she has great potential, but she has more than I expected. I don't want to get my hopes up. Until the last test is done. I know you are trying to stop her mom, but I like her already. There is no one who can stop love. Even though I wield it, I cannot fully control it," says a gruff and tired voice.

There is a commotion at the office door as Max bursts into the room, with the secretary right behind him trying to hold him back from entering the room.

"Why is Janan lying on the couch? What are you doing to her? Making her work all night after work? What made her faint?" Max demands as he walks into the room.

I sit up slowly to get up, not wanting to stay here. I want to go home. Away from this weird family. If they were family or some ancient Greek cult. I am done. Eros wasn't coming back and his mother, I guess his mother, is just having fun with me. "What are you doing here, Max?" I feel a heaviness in my body.

"I saw you walk in and go up to this office. Why are you lying down?"

"I'm ok Max. Let's leave. I'm ready to leave."

Max helps me get up, and we walk towards the door. Eros is standing just inside the office door. I didn't know he was here. So much for his attention when I am down. "Why are you leaving with that man? You have unfinished business with me and my mother. If you leave now, you might not get what you want. All this would be for nothing."

"I don't know what you are going on about. I tried to contact you but nothing. And then I end up seeing your mother who sends me on these tests. You finally show up and it's me who will cause us to not talk? Where were you? I'm leaving with a friend. Someone I can count on being there even while he's angry at me. That's more than you did."

"I can't share everything, but I was with you and I tried to help where I could. I had hoped that you would pass my mother's tests. Please don't leave now. Let's have that talk we need to have. The one we should have had when I left."

"Hey you, I don't care if you're our boss, but you haven't been here for her, I have. You don't treat women properly. Let's go, Janan, he's not good enough for you." Max shouts.

I could tell Max cares for me, and he is trying to defend and support me. But he isn't my guy. He doesn't understand that I could finally talk to Eros. Not being able to pass up that moment to talk, no matter how angry I was. I need to tell Eros how I feel, not just storm off as I wasn't a damsel in distress, needing to flee the scene. I am a woman who is ready to fight for myself. Whether that would mean getting back together with Eros or standing up for myself, is yet to be decided.

Chapter 17

"Thanks for your support, Max, but I need to talk to Daniel. This conversation is necessary." I decide, staring at Eros.

"How could you still want to talk to him? He's no good for you."

"Thank you, but you should go. I need to talk to him. What I decide to do after that is up to me. I appreciate your support, but I need to do this."

Max shakes his head and looks hurt. He leaves without another word. I know in that instant he saw me as a failed romance and that I was a lost cause. I am not the girl for him. But I wasn't a lost cause either. I still haven't decided on whether Eros is the right guy for me. This time I won't be blind. I would see his expressions as I talked to him. I'd see if he is earnest as he sounds or a liar.

"Let's talk then Eros" I declare, straightening up to hide the after effects of fainting. I don't want to be seen as weak.

Zoe and the secretary leave to give us some privacy. As Zoe walks past me, she says, "you have potential, but I still don't think you're good enough. You will only hurt him in the end."

"Well, I still have to see if he is good enough for me as well, so I guess we are even." I retort. Like only Eros' feelings mattered. What about mine?

I walk over to one couch and sit down. Eros went to sit opposite of me on the other couch so we were facing each other. "So I see you and Max are close now." Eros stares daggers at me.

"Don't do that. Max is just a friend to me. Don't bring him into this. This is about us. And I should start by saying sorry for breaking our agreement by looking at you when we were blind dating. But I also think it's unfair that you knew exactly who I was the whole time. And you just left, and I have had no contact from you since Tuesday night. It's now Friday. You just ghosted me for three days and that is not ok." Staring right back at him, I hold my ground.

"I'm sorry I just left. But you don't understand. If I'm not careful, you might get hurt if you see who I am, as I have to be in control of how you see me. I know that makes little sense right now, but I will explain it one day. I was also hurt because I really thought you trusted me." Eros looks at the floor.

"I did trust you, but I really wanted to see you and I don't understand what you mean when you say you have to control how I see you as I'm looking at you now, and it's fine. I know who you are and I'm ok."

"Right now, I am acting as Daniel. But that is an alias, it's not my real name. Eros is my real name. I can't tell you more right now, but I hope you can trust me enough to see this through. One day, I will tell you everything. But I need to know you can handle it. That is why we are going slow. I don't want to hurt you. I want you to be fully aware of who I am and to make your own choice about us being together. But this will take time." He looks up at me and reaches out a hand towards me. I don't reach back, so his hand falls beside him.

"Are you in a cult? Or the mafia? Or in hiding? I don't get this at all."

"No, I'm not into anything like that. But it's complicated." Eros retorts and leans back angrily.

"How can I trust you will open up one day? How can I trust you to stay and not just disappear on me again?" I push, staring at him.

"I understand how hard this is for you. How unfair it is that I am asking you to trust me when you are so open about yourself and I'm not telling you anything about myself. But you have such potential, I think I will be able to share everything with you, eventually." He says with his voice rising in hope.

"Why do you and your mother both keep saying I have potential? What does that even mean?"

He sits up. "It means a great deal. That I will tell you everything and maybe we can have a happy ever after."

"But your mother doesn't like me. She says I'll hurt you."

Leaning towards me he says, "I haven't found the one who could be my happily ever after. I thought I found it once before, but she couldn't be my forever as she died. I hope you will be able to do what she could not."

"What do you mean? I'm sorry you lost her, but I don't know how I can be any better as we all die, eventually." I lean a bit backwards, wanting the clarity that some space would give me.

"There is so much to tell you, but I can't yet. I need my mother's permission. You have to have great potential. I'm sorry, but there will be another test you must pass. A dangerous one."

I stand up. "I don't like these tests, and I don't understand why you need your mother's permission. You're an adult, aren't you?"

Eros stands up and grabs my arm, stopping me from leaving. "Yes, but this is the way it must be done. You are passing every test. I will be with you for the last test. And I will tell you the dangers when we come to it. You will still have to return the box to my mother as she left without it. She will probably hide from you, so you will have to think about where you can find her."

"I brought it to her. Why do I have to do so again?"

"I'm sorry but this must be done."

"What if I think this is too much and don't do it?"

"Of course, you may stop at any time, but it means we will no longer be together."

"Are we together now? You left." I spit, jerking the arm he was holding.

"I'm sorry I left, and I won't suddenly leave again and disappear. I want to trust you with my heart and I truly believe we will find happiness together. I'm all in, are you?"

"I want to trust you, Eros. I want to be happy with you. But I don't like these tests. I don't like how I have to wait for information about you." I say tiredly. The effects of the day are still weighing me down.

"I know. I'm sorry, but it must be done this way. The elders are so ancient they make it hard for me to find love. But they do it this way so that we do not hurt anyone in the end. These tests are to make sure you can handle the last one." He gently caresses my face with his other hand.

"This is a lot to take in." Feeling his hand on my face calms me down. *This isn't fair.*

"Yes. This is why we must do the process slowly. To give you time to adapt to our way of life."

"Will we still date the same as before, or will we be dating publicly?" I demand. There was no way I'd go back to dating in private. I want a genuine relationship.

"I can take you out in public now. But first, you must find my mother and give her the box. While you do that, I'll go to the leader of the elders and ask for his help with my mom."

"What's his name?"

"Zeus."

"Of course. And you aren't in a cult, right?" I say, stepping out of his hands. His hands fall beside him.

"No. We just use old names in private. Only the family knows these names. Everyone else only knows our public names. Mine is Daniel right now."

"Right now?"

"Yes. I move often and change my name to suit the place."

"Oh boy. That is unusual. How long do you plan on staying in Vancouver?"

"Hopefully for a long time, with you." He smiles.

"Ok, that's good to hear. So you are treating me like family?" He reaches to hold my hand, entwining our fingers. The electricity is always there between us. *Is this his secret weapon?*

"Yes. I came intending to have you join my family. That is why I gave you my real name."

CHAPTER 17

"Ok. Let's try this. I'll give this box to Zoe. Then we can date normally?"

"Yes. I'll get back up from Zeus so my mom can be more positive. We need Zeus' approval to be together. So if I can get him on our side, that would help placate my mother."

"Any hints where I might find her?"

"I do not know where she might go. But if you think about it I'm sure you'll find her. Think of her real name."

"Sure Aphrodite right?"

"Yes, I don't know how you got her name, but it will give you a hand in dealing with her."

"I want a great first public date for all of this trouble." I demand.

"Definitely." he chuckles.

Chapter 18

Where would she be? Where would Aphrodite go in Vancouver? Somewhere for love? No, that's not quite right. Aphrodite represents lust more than love. So where would lusty lovers go? I pull out my phone and open Google Maps. I search for lust…no luck, just a thrift store. Well, that didn't help. A strip joint? Well, that brought out some leads. But none of the places sound or look right. Oh, what about Victoria's Secret, as I saw it on Google Maps, there is one close by on Robson Street. I walk over and look around, but can't find her. Wait, what about Burlesque? That has some hits, too. Oh, there was a cabaret place that is close by and looks fancy enough for Aphrodite. And it's open on Fridays in the early afternoon. I'll try it. Finding their number, I call the cabaret. An employee answers and says they can't say if someone is there or not. They respect their clientele's privacy. I thank them and go see for myself.

Reaching the cabaret, I walk in and the bouncer asks to see my ID. Fumbling in my purse, I eventually find it. I give it to him and he lets me in. I am directed to a seat by the wall on the right by the hostess. Trying to look around for Aphrodite, I can't seem to get a good look. There are lots of people and the show is just starting up. The dancers are so confident and fierce. I love their attitude. Once the show is over, people mingle. I take my chance and walk around the place until I find Aphrodite in an alcove by the stage. I summon some courage and walk over to her.

"Hi Zoe, I have your box for you. You seemed to have forgotten it when you left."

"Oh Janan, you found me. How did you do that?"

"Well, I asked myself where would Aphrodite go? And my luck brought me here."

"Well done, sit. I'll take that off your hands."

"Thanks."

"I want you to know I don't dislike you. It's just that I am trying to protect my son. He is easily hurt. He cares deeply."

"I have no intention of hurting him."

"I know. But we move every five to ten years, and he leaves behind loved ones and it hurts him. The big love of his life lived with us for a short time and died. He was hurt for so long. I don't want him to go through that again."

"He mentioned her to me. I know he cares deeply. Why do you move every five to ten years?"

"I can't tell you that yet. But it's a nice change of pace. It helps to keep life interesting. The adventure."

"I can see how that is adventurous. A fresh start and all that. But do you leave everyone behind? Or do some people move with you?"

"Only very special people move with us. Ones who are knowledgeable. We have family traditions that make it hard for people to get close to us."

"I think I'm getting to know how hard it is, through all of these tests you and Eros have put me through."

"You have potential, but I doubt you'll pass the last test. Very few do. The last love of Eros didn't pass the test, and that is why she eventually died."

"I don't understand any of this, but I do know I want to be with your son. I will try to do my best."

"I hope you succeed. Then my son can be truly happy. But I don't have high hopes, many do not pass. It is your fate and only the Moirai know your fate."

"If I pass this test, can I stay with Eros indefinitely?"

"Yes, if you choose that fate. But you should choose the man who helped you on your tests. He will make you happy and you would not have to deal with our family traditions. It would be a safer love and life."

"Then I will try the test. I don't want anyone other than Eros."

"It's very dangerous, you could hurt yourself. We shall see if you get the chance. Go see Eros. You don't have a lot of time left together. We will be moving in a few months."

"You are? So soon? Why didn't he tell me that?"

"Go be with Eros."

I leave and call Eros, but he doesn't answer. Maybe he is still talking with Zeus. I decide to go home and eat. I have hardly eaten today. And I could rest while Eros talks to Zeus. I am still feeling a little fragile after fainting.

Chapter 19

I wake up the next morning feeling refreshed. A good meal and early night in are exactly what I needed. I look at my phone to see a text from Eros inviting me on a date. *Are you free today? Let's meet by The Drop beside Canada Place. Dress casual-dressy.*

Intrigued, I look through my closet, wondering how casual or how dressy I should be. I find a pair of low leopard heels, a pair of black slacks, a white blouse, a tan cardigan, a long gold necklace and bangles, and a medium brown purse I could put across my chest with the strap. Perfect. Wondering how long we might walk, I put a pair of black flats into my purse. They just fit. I can't wait to be on an actual date outside with Eros.

As it is a thirty-minute walk to Canada Place from my place, I take an Uber so I can walk further with Eros in my heels. It is a quick ride, and I arrive there in minutes. As I usually do, I get there early. I walk to The Drop and look out at the water. A seaplane is landing, and it is fun to watch. A hand falls on my shoulder, startling me. I turn around to find Eros standing behind me in a white Oxford button-down shirt, light gray slacks, and black loafers. We match each other very well.

"Eros! You startled me!" I say, laughing.

"Sorry, I just couldn't wait for the plane to finish landing. You look so beautiful with your dark brown hair flowing behind you."

"Well, you look like quite the catch today as well. How did we know to dress similarly?"

"We have similar tastes. I like it."

"What's on the agenda today?"

"It's a surprise. Follow me and let's go on an adventure. This way." He guides my elbow towards the north and we walked side by side along the seawall towards Stanley Park. Taking my hand and putting it in the crook of his arm, he says, "Do you like waterfalls?"

"Oh yes, I do. They are so breathtaking."

"Great. Then you will like the first stop on our tour."

"A tour. Oh, we have a day planned." I say excitedly.

"Right about here. We will go up this way a bit."

"Are you taking me to a hotel?"

"Yes, and no."

Walking past the entrance of the hotel, there is a green patch that has trees surrounding a water feature with stone steps to step over the water and a bench to sit on. "Oh, this is lovely!"

We sit down on the bench and watch the water for a few minutes.

"I know it might be early, but I feel like it's been a long time coming. Would you be my girlfriend?" Eros asks.

I think for a minute, thinking about all I've been through. It all came down to trust. I want to trust Eros so badly and live in the moment, so I decide to trust him about who he is and his family rules. He will tell me what I need to know when it's time. "How romantic. Yes! I would."

Eros reaches for me and kisses me gently. We are savoring each other. There is no rush. But I have a sliver of thought that makes me pull away. He is leaving in a few months. This would not last. He would leave me all over again, but this time permanently if what his mother said was true.

"What's wrong Janan?"

CHAPTER 19

"In a few months, you will leave Vancouver. Your mother told me. Will you leave me behind just as we officially start to date?"

"I don't want to leave you, Janan. I will stay here longer, but I will eventually have to leave, and I would want to take you with me. In the end, It's your decision to be with me and my family's acceptance that is also needed."

"I would want to go with you. I get your family is different. Why would I need their permission?"

"If you come, you will learn our secrets. So you will need to be part of the family. Not anyone can become part of our family. That is why we have the tests. To see if you will make the transition into our family."

"I will take whatever tests are needed."

"That means the world to me. I want to tell you everything. But I must point out that the likelihood of you passing is very slim, as it would be for anyone. If you decide not to do the test or fail, I will stay with you as long as I can, but that would probably only be for five years."

"I don't get that at all. I don't understand why you have to move. You promise you're not the mafia or something?"

"We are not the mafia. But my family has our traditions and secrets. It's because we age so slowly, people get uncomfortable with us and this is why we move a lot. I'm sorry I can't be more clear."

"What do you mean, you age so slowly? I don't get it," I say, sitting up.

"My family lives a long time, too long for most people to understand. I'm saying too much as it is."

"You're not saying enough. You are not being clear. I don't understand what you are trying to explain. This aging thing is an excuse, isn't it? To leave me behind in the future?"

"Definitely not. I want to be with you always. If you pass, then you will be able to join my family, we can be together forever.

"I will take as many as needed, but how many are left? Aren't the ones I took already enough? Why is it so hard to join your family?"

"I don't know how many more tests you need to do. This will be up to Zeus. I tried to explain the situation to him and he agreed that we will proceed, but I don't know what he has planned. It's out of my hands. Zeus is the boss of the family and I cannot go against him if he decides you're not worthy enough. But I would stay with you until Zeus says I have to leave you."

"What do you mean, Zeus will decide everything? That is crazy."

"I want us to become a family. I want to be with you always. This is why I went to Zeus. He will come and see you are worthy of becoming family. My mother will try to keep us apart because she is worried I will experience the pain of losing someone else I love and care about."

"I guess I'll just have to wait and believe in your process."

"I have high hopes. I love you so much."

"You love me? Oh, I love you too."

I pull Eros in for a kiss, tasting his lips and then nipping at them. Opening Eros's mouth, I play with our tongues, taking him inside my mouth and sucking it. Wanting more of him inside me.

"Wait," He says, pulling back, "there's still the rest of our date. We can continue this later." He pulls me to my feet as he stands up. "This way, my lady."

We continue to walk towards Stanley Park on the seawall. I love taking in the views of the water and boats. We come to the beginning of Stanley Park and walk a little way in. There is a blanket with a basket on it under a tree in the sun. It is a nice day out, not that hot with a warm breeze. The picnic spot couldn't be more perfect. "Is this for us?" I ask.

"It is. Have a seat and I'll get lunch ready." He takes out some napkins and boxes of bite-sized food and puts the boxes between us. Now we can reach the food equally.

"This looks so delicious! Did you make it?"

"I did. I love cooking. Try everything. It all goes well together."

"Oh yummy," I can't resist, everything looks so delicious, "I could get used to this."

"I will pleasure you with my body and food. Don't you worry, there will be plenty of both." He says, laughing.

When I am done, I lay down on the blanket, soaking up the sun. "I could stay here like this for a long time."

CHAPTER 19

"I'm glad you are enjoying yourself, but we are not done. Take a short rest and then we will move on to the next item on our agenda."

"There's more? Well, I'd better rest up then. Come here next to me."

Eros finishes putting the boxes away and comes and lies beside me. I move, so I am leaning on his chest in the crook of his shoulder. It is bliss.

After a short while, Eros rubs my arms. "It's time to get up. We have another place to go."

"This is perfect. We could just stay here."

"Trust me, you don't want to miss the next event!"

"It must be something amazing," I laugh, "alright, let's go."

We leave the basket and blanket behind and walk along Denman to English Bay, then south to Sunset Beach. There is Latin music playing in the parking lot. "Are we dancing?!" I ask.

"Yes. Do you like Latin dancing?"

"I do. It's so fun but I'm a beginner, so please be gentle."

"Don't worry, you will look like a proficient dancer with me."

"This is awesome! This whole day is magical, thank you!"

"I'm glad you are enjoying it. Let's dance." Luckily I have my flats, so I change into them quickly. I want to make full use of this random dance party to have some fun with Eros.

We dance for several hours. Dancing is fun, and it is making me so horny. Being close to him and feeling his heat as we dance is such a turn-on. As the song ends, I hug Eros in close and lean up to him and say, "this has been amazing. I'm ready to leave, though."

"Why do you want to leave?"

"Because I want you. I can't wait any longer."

"Oh, I see. Let's go. My place is a bit far, but it shouldn't take too long to get there."

"Let's go to mine. It's close by."

"Sure, that sounds great. Lead the way."

I direct him up to Beach Avenue and then up the hill towards Davie Street, then down one street to the south. In a few minutes, we are outside my place. "Here it is."

"I'm excited to see your place."

"I'm excited to have you there, inside." I laugh at the cheesy line.

"You will be satisfied, my lady." He chuckles, pulling me in for a quick kiss.

We make our way up the elevator, hugging and kissing the whole way. We manage to open my door and go inside. The entrance is wide, with the living room right in front of the door. The kitchen is to the left. And the bathroom and bedroom are to the right. I decorated it in a minimalist style with Ikea furniture. It isn't very fashionable, but it is workable. "I see we are both minimalists. Only keeping a few keepsakes as memories. It helps when you move a lot."

"Yes, exactly. Well, hopefully you won't be moving too soon."

"No, I will be here for a while yet."

I pull him towards the bedroom by his hand. Needing to feel the connection between us as we walk, I link our fingers together. I walk into the bedroom and I push Eros onto the bed, making him sit at the edge, wanting to be in control. I straddle him and kiss him softly at first, then with more passion. He pulls me more into him, strengthening my desire. Feeling his growing passion, I rub myself on him. His hands are around my back, but then one hand moves down to grab my butt, squeezing it. Eros falls backward, and he rolls us around so that he is on top. I like the way he takes control over me, making me wetter as his weight pushes me into the bed. With my legs still around him, he comes in and kisses me. One of his hands cups my breast and squeezes it. Wanting to see all of him, I reach for his shirt, unbuttoning it from top to bottom. He shrugs his shirt off and he is nicely muscled. He gazes down at me. "You are so beautiful, you don't even know."

"Thanks," I say, blushing.

"You even blush. How cute are you!"

He comes in for another kiss and pulls off my cardigan. Once it is free, he pulls off my shirt. I reach for the zipper on his pants, sliding it down. Taking off his pants, he shows me all of him at once, as he isn't wearing any underwear.

CHAPTER 19

Beautiful and strong. He is magnificent. All I could ever want. He is very aroused, and I want to feel him inside me. He pulls my pants off and looks at me. "So beautiful. I will worship you." Removing my bra, he begins by kissing my neck. Then he moves down to my breasts, kissing and squeezing them. As he is kneeling between my legs, I push myself up and against him. He makes me feel so wet. He growls and says, "Oh, not yet. I need to worship you first." Removing my panties, he lowers himself between my legs. He takes his thumb and begins touching my clitoris. His warmth heats me up real good. Then he lowers his head and uses his tongue and mouth, licking and sucking me. I feel very warm. Then three of his fingers go inside me and I begin to moan and ride his fingers. I keep rising and rising in pleasure until I burst with a very loud moan. I let myself fall back down as Eros still licks and fingers me. It feels so good.

I pull him up to me and kiss him deeply, pulling his tongue inside my mouth and sucking it. I can taste myself on him and it makes me want him more. It is my turn to please him and I can't wait to do it. I push him onto his back with a grin on my face. "You worshiped me very well, now it's my turn." I lift his cock and rub him down with my hands and then I put the tip in my mouth and lick it, working my way lower until I had it all in my mouth. I suck it and move up and down with my hands below my mouth. He is watching with bright eyes and his head tilts back in pleasure. He moans as I worship him and he pulls me up suddenly and is holding himself back. "Oh, that was so good, Janan. I almost came, but I want to be inside you. Can I come inside you?"

"Yes. I have birth control and condoms. I want to feel you inside me as well, and your release."

Moaning, he says, "You are so wonderful." I give him the condom, and he pulls me to lie down and puts himself over me and between my legs. He leans forward to kiss me and we rub ourselves together until his tip is just outside, slightly penetrating me. He slowly pushes it in. It feels like ecstasy. I mold myself around him, stretching to fit him in, I relish the pleasure. Soon he is all the way inside and it feels better than any lover I've had before. "You feel so perfect Janan."

"You fill me so well, Eros. You feel so good."

He moves slowly at first, then faster. He grabs my hips so he can go faster and deeper. My head hits the headboard, but I don't care. All I can feel is Eros. We rise higher and higher in pleasure until I burst. I come around him and he moans and thrusts hard and fast, then comes himself. I can feel his eruption. It feels so good, it increases my pleasure from my orgasm. Once it is over, he holds himself still inside me. I don't want him to leave. He slowly pulls out and lays down beside me, pulling me down so I am leaning into the crook of his shoulder on top of his chest. We both lay there in ecstasy as the pleasure slowly leaves us.

Chapter 20

The next morning, Eros wakes me up by kissing my neck. "Good morning," he whispers.

I look at him and smile. He is shining. "Good morning, handsome. The sun makes you look so bright." He smiles but doesn't reply and kisses me instead, a nice long sweet kiss. He pulls away saying, "I have to call Zeus today. Hopefully, he will help me get my mom to accept you so we can do the test. I know you will pass it if you see so much through the fog."

"What fog?"

"I promise to explain everything after all this is done."

"Ok, I trust you."

"It means so much that you do. I love you."

"I love you. Even though I know so little, I want to know more. I feel apprehensive about all this, but I want to go through with it."

He kisses me one more time, then gets up and gets dressed. "See you later, my lady."

"See you later. Good luck."

He leaves my place, and I lay there wondering what he and his mother said about what I saw and the potential they see in me. I wonder what that was all about. Deciding I would not dwell on it, I get up and get dressed. Since I have the day to myself, I decide to head over to my sister's place to catch her up to what's been going on. I dress casually in light blue jeans and a green T-shirt. Put on some sneakers and grab my bag from yesterday and head to her place.

It is a pleasant walk. The sun is shining and the cherry trees are still in bloom. When I get there, I buzz her number. "Who is it?" Chloe asks.

"Me!" I say laughing.

"Oh, Janan! Come right up."

When I get to her door, she's already there waiting for me. She rushes out and hugs me. She is shorter than me and so when we hug, her head is near my shoulder, with her long black hair flowing around her. Her dark brown eyes were smiling along with her mouth. "I feel like it's been so long since I last saw you."

"Sorry for being MIA these past weeks. But I came to see you and give you an update about my life."

"Oh, I can't wait for the news." Showing me inside, we went to the balcony like usual. She has already placed drinks and snacks on the table.

"How did you know I was coming?" I ask.

"I didn't, but I was getting ready for a read-a-thon on the balcony already. So I just added another glass when you buzzed me on the intercom." She says laughing.

"Good timing!" We sit and chat a bit. Then Chloe goes in for the kill. "So tell me all about him! Is he a creep or are you in love?" Laughing, I answer "I'm in love. I found out who he is. He's my boss Daniel Lennon, CEO of Matchmaker. That's part of the reason he hid who he was. It's ok to date within the company, but I did just start there and he is in charge. That might have been why he was so secretive. Plus, his family is weird about their traditions, but I think they have good intentions. I met his mother. I don't know if she likes me, but it's clear no one would be good enough for her son. So that might be a battle I'll have to tackle later. First, there's this test I must take."

"A test? What are they, rich snobs? I don't like that you have to do a test to be with him."

"I don't either, but I love him and I want to try."

"Well, I'll support you, but if he hurts you, I will not let him get away from my wrath."

"Thanks, sis. It means a lot. Now tell me about your life." We chat the day away, laughing, and talking about our lives the past few weeks. It was nice to have a normal day talking with my sister. How I missed her, I didn't realize it had been so long since I talked to her.

Later that evening, as I walk back to my place from Chloe's, I feel like everything is going well. I feel loved by my sister and Eros. I don't want to take it for granted. My phone dings, I've gotten a text. Checking it, I see it's from Eros. *Please come to my office. Zeus and I have convinced my mother to test you. We have deemed you worthy.* I am glad I was worthy, but I didn't like how that makes them sound. Like they are above me. It annoys me. I know I am still going to meet up with them and I know Eros isn't looking down at me. I would do this test and throw my value in their faces.

As I get to Eros's office, I see the door is open, so I go in. Sitting on the couches are Zoe and Eros. A giant muscular man with gray hair wearing a business suit sitting in the seat saved for the CEO. I guess this is Zeus, and he is in charge. "Hi, I'm Janan. Nice to meet you, Zeus."

"Welcome Janan. Please have a seat." Replies Zeus.

"Thank you." I sit next to Eros, facing his mother.

"You know Eros can only live with you for five years, right? Do you still choose him with these conditions?" Zeus asks.

"Yes. I want to be with Eros. Even with whatever time we have. I would like to be with him for a lifetime, but I understand you move a lot. I don't mind traveling."

"If you stay with Eros, you would lose your family. Would you be able to handle that?"

"I want keep in touch with my sister. It's just the two of us. I love her and she will be part of my family in the future as well."

"I see you do not understand. You have to give up your sister if you stay with Eros for over five years."

"I will always stay in contact with my sister."

"You may stay in touch but you will miss her physically as you cannot see her in real life after 5 years if you succeed. This is usually the hardest part for mortals." Zeus explains.

"I don't understand why I have to give up my sister."

"You don't have to lose her altogether, but there will be a point in time where you won't be able to see her. You must think about this, you will lose everything you know to be with Eros. Do you agree with this?"

"I love Eros and I want to be with him for as long as I can. But I love my sister as well. It's just the two of us."

"You must decide what is most important to you." He says kindly.

It is the hardest decision of my life. I want to be with Eros. But I can't live without my sister. It's been just the two of us for so long. Our parents died in our twenties and it's just been the two of us since then. How could I just leave her? I wouldn't be fully leaving her, just not able to see her in person. It bothers me so much. But the love I have with Eros is unimaginable. I don't want to be without him, either. But Chloe would understand. Wouldn't she?

Chapter 21

"I have decided that I want to do the test and be with Eros, even if I lose my family."

"Well done. You can now go to the next step." Zeus announces.

"That's great Janan! I knew you could do it!" Eros exclaims.

"We shall see if she passes the final one." Aphrodite says.

"What is the last test?" I ask.

Ignoring me, Zeus tells Eros, "she can only be with you for five years. She has faith but not enough potential. We three are here and she sees nothing. I've changed my mind, I do not think she will survive."

What do you mean, I see nothing? I think. I look closer at Zeus. He seems to pulse with energy. Even his hair looks like it has static electricity. But otherwise, he looks like a normal man. Except he is super fit. "Do you mean I don't see the static electricity on you?"

"Very good Janan," says Eros, smiling.

"Is that all you see?" Zeus demands.

"Well, you're very fit for a man with white and gray hair." I reply.

"You see white hair? Oh, you can see my age, interesting. What other things have you seen that are not normal?"

I don't know what he means, so I stare at him, thinking.

"Oh, she's seen Eros' wings," Aphrodite replies, "tell them what you saw, Janan," Aphrodite says.

"Well, the day I spied on you while you were sleeping, I saw golden wings behind you. I was still dreaming, wasn't I?"

"Golden? Psyche only saw white, but you saw golden, which means she might have more potential than Psyche." Zeus says. "What else have you seen?"

"Well, I looked in the box and saw the golden arrow. But I passed out after that."

"You saw the arrow and then passed out. You have a strong will. That's important. You can see beyond the fog even when we throw it at you," Zeus commends me.

"She also saw me glowing this morning. She said I was bright like the sun." Helps Eros.

"You are an interesting girl," Zeus says. "I have decided that you may proceed to the final step. But you must know what that means. It means that you will lose your sister and friends. You will always move from place to place, never setting down roots and you will make friendships that will only last a few years before you must give them up and move again. You will have all the time in the world but be distant from regular life. But, you will have us, your family. We have many traditions you will have to learn. Once you choose this fate, there is no going back. What do you say?"

"I want to be with Eros. My sister will understand. It will be nice to be part of a large family. I haven't had a big family in so long, it has been just my sister and I for some time now."

"Then it is time to tell you what family you will join," Zeus continues. "You would be part of a family of gods. We are immortals from ancient times. Our names live on in myth, but we hide who we are from mortals, as they would not be able to understand us any longer. We live for eternity and it is very hard to kill us. We have powers that mortals would fear, so we hide in our glamor magic. This is the fog that came out of the box. It makes mortals weak, so they do not see beyond what they should. Our powers vary from god to god. But we all shine with ancient power and live eternally. Would you like to join this family?"

CHAPTER 21

"You are gods? Like the original ancient Greek gods? Are you trying to prank me?"

"Yes, I know it's out there, but it's true. You saw some of my powers. Do you not believe us? What he says is true." Eros says.

"I think I need a minute...isn't there a Psyche that married Eros?"

"Yes, she was my only wife. We had a daughter together. She couldn't become a god as she didn't have enough potential. She lived a longer-than-normal lifespan because of the ambrosia, and she lived for 150 years. But she eventually died from old age. It was heartbreaking. I loved her so much." Eros answers.

"He was heartbroken for centuries. I do not trust you with his heart, as you could do the same to him. I do not want to see him lose another love," Aphrodite says.

"You're really gods? Show me, please."

"If we show ourselves fully, you will die, mortal. But we can lift the mist a little for you to believe us," Zeus says. Staring at them, I see them glow. Aphrodite has a pink mist around her head. Zeus has electricity in the air. Eros has his golden wings. They are actual gods. I can't believe what I am seeing. "Oh my gosh, you are gods!"

Zeus laughs. "That didn't take long. You can see past the mist easily. This means things might go well for you. Do you want to become a god, Janan?"

Chapter 22

"Am I able to become a god? How is that possible?" I ask.

"Well, there is a way to do it. But it might not work." warns Zeus.

"Is that how you became gods?"

"No, we were born gods. But we have found Ambrosia that lifts our powers and can turn some mortals into gods. Probably those with distant relations to gods. And you seem to be one of the few who might be able to turn into a god."

"Oh wow. This is why I'd have to leave my sister? Is there a chance she could become a god as well? She probably has the same potential as I do."

"We are selecting you because of Eros. Your sister might not be eligible, sometimes it skips family members. First, you must decide whether to be a god. The fate of your sister is her own and she must follow her own journey."

"I see. I want to be a god. And if possible, test my sister once I've become a god."

"You may fail. Do not get ahead of yourself," rebukes Zeus. "It's we who decide who to test."

"Yes, I'm sorry, but my sister is all I have and I am all she has."

"You have Eros now. And possibly his family. Your sister will have her own family, eventually."

"I suppose so, but it wouldn't be the same."

"I see you care deeply for your sister. For your sake and my peace of mind, I will think about testing her as well. But first, you must pass the test."

"Oh thank you, Zeus!"

"Do not thank me yet, mortal. The test is not an easy one. And it has many dangers."

"What kind of dangers?" I ask.

"You may experience hallucinations, delirium, or death. It is not a pleasant test, it will test the ability of your mind to surpass reality and see beyond the mist. It will determine if your mind and body can handle immortality."

"You can do it Janan! I know you'll make it." Eros says. "But to let you know, Psyche didn't pass this test. She could handle the ambrosia, but it only made her live a little longer. She could not transition fully into a god. But you see more than she did. You can handle seeing beyond the mist more clearly."

"The test is to take ambrosia?"

"Yes," Eros confirms.

"What is ambrosia? Chocolate?"

"No, it's not chocolate, that's just clever advertising," Eros says. "It's actually a type of mushroom."

"Really mushrooms? I see how they could make you hallucinate, but how do they make you immortal?"

"Demeter made it long ago. She cultivated a few special blends of mushrooms and used her knowledge and powers to create the mushrooms of immortality called ambrosia." Zeus explains, "It is a powerful mushroom and is dangerous to all who are not immortal. Demeter only knows its full powers. And she guards them well. It is she who gave us the tests to make sure we do not kill too many mortals. Also, I limit how many can take the tests as there can be only so many immortals. Too many and we would ruin the earth. We live a very long time."

"Thank you for letting me have a chance to be with Eros. Together for lifetimes sounds nice."

"Oh, you just wait, there will be decades where you don't get along but in the end, we love our partners as only they can understand us with this type of life," Zeus says laughing, "family is everything to us. Even though we fight sometimes,

CHAPTER 22

we are a tight-knit group. You must understand this marriage will be forever. You must be dedicated enough to survive it."

"I love Eros and I would be happy to live lifetimes with him. It would be great to be part of a big family. I want to become a god. I am scared I will have side effects from the ambrosia, but I still want to try it."

"It's normal to be scared. It means you fully understand the circumstances and are not just thinking about the power of being a god. You are here for the right reasons. This is also why you've been able to pass our tests so far," Zeus compliments me, "but before we prepare for the ceremony, there is one last thing to do."

Chapter 23

"Please come this way Janan." Zeus leads me to another room that has mirrors all around on the walls.

"What's this room for?" I ask.

"There's one more step before you become a god, this is very important. You must do what I tell you to do. Any deviation and you will fail. Understood?"

"Yes, I'll do exactly what you tell me," I reply.

"You will look directly into my eyes when I say to look at me. Nowhere else or you will die. Eros will react, but you cannot say or do anything else but look into my eyes. Understood?"

Straightening up, I say "yes."

"Good. Aphrodite, you can come in now."

In comes Aphrodite and Eros, on the other side of the room.

"Why is Zeus with Janan?" Eros asks worriedly.

"Hush boy, let him do his test," Aphrodite says.

Zeus says, "now we shall see if she has the full potential for becoming a god. Watch boy, as she undergoes this test. She will be the last woman that I will ever test for you. If she is not worthy, you will never ask me again for this test," turning to me Zeus says, "now look at me and see what God's are made of."

I look into Zeus's eyes and wait. There is a bright light around him, but I don't look anywhere else but his eyes. Suddenly Eros screams, "No! She can't see you without the mist! She will die! Stop!"

Zeus says quietly, "make sure to look directly at my eyes."

There is a thump as Eros falls to the floor screaming, "no! You killed her! She couldn't take it. She wasn't a god yet. How could you?" He wails in agony. "I loved her! She's the only one in eons that I've felt something for and you killed her."

As Eros cries into the floor, Zeus tells me quietly, "look into my eyes or die for real. We are not done yet."

All I can hear is Eros sobbing. It breaks my heart. I want to go to him, tell him I am alive. But if I do, we would fail the test. And I might die. I want to be with Eros but I can't take this deception. If he needs me now, I have to go to him. I can't let him suffer for no reason. Closing my eyes, I turn and run to Eros. Hoping I won't die for real. I grab him in a hug and yell, "it's OK, I'm ok. I am here."

Eros looks up at me and returns my hug, holding me close, saying, "you're OK, you're OK." We cling desperately to each other as Aphrodite says "Well, you have failed the test. Now he really will see you die one day. This is his future. This is why I don't like you."

Eros stands up and faces his mother. "Does this make you happy? My misery? I am the god of love and you wish me a life without the happiness that comes from love? You revel in the carnal experience of love, but have you ever felt genuine love? Do you want to see me unfulfilled in my duty, even to myself? I am a man. I do not let anyone control me, you least of all. You will respect me or you will never see me again. You will no longer be part of my family."

"Strong words for a strong man, but she is your weakness and will cause you unnecessary strife."

"Enough. Both of you. Now hear my verdict," Zeus says, "she did not fail this test. This test was for Eros. He passed by expressing the depths of his love for her and Janan proved herself worthy by disobeying me, and risking her life to

CHAPTER 23

comfort Eros. They have a genuine love match, so they may be married. There is only the ceremony left to see if she survives the transition.

Aphrodite, Eros, and Janan look at Zeus as if he's crazy. Eros starts, "it looked so real. Her looking at you and exploding from the energy. I couldn't bear it."

Zeus says, "I can make you see what I want. She listened very well to avoid dying for real when she closed her eyes. I knew she was part of our family. You have to listen to your elders, but you must also listen to your heart if you want to be a worthy god. She is worthy. And you are worthy of her."

Chapter 24

I sit with Eros, holding hands, waiting for the ceremony to begin. Just me and Eros are still in his office on the couch. My hands shake a little, but Eros smooths my hands with his, gently squeezing them. "It's ok, I will be with you the whole time. I will look after you. You will be fine, I know it. I can't believe you see so much through the mist." Eros says. He pulls me in for a hug, and I cradle my head between his shoulder and neck. Reminding myself how much I love this man, even though it's been a short time, I feel like he is my fate. The one I belong with.

Aphrodite comes into the room, "We are ready for the ceremony. Please come this way."

We get up and follow her to the events room. As we enter the room, there is a man softly playing the lyre, alternating banners of dolphins with blue backgrounds and roosters with red backgrounds, and torches aflame with roses around their staff. The front of the room is an arbor full of roses and a bed on the other side under a flag of a bow pulled taught with an arrow. All these elements spoke of Eros' attributes as a god. This is more than just a ceremony for me to turn into a god; this is more like a wedding.

"Eros, what is this ceremony?"

"You will take the ambrosia, and we shall stay here while you undergo its effects. You also agree to be mine, my wife, that is."

"Oh Eros, I'm not dressed properly."

"It's not about how you dress, it's about your intentions. We are both ready to pledge to be with one another. There is no more powerful commitment than becoming a god for one another."

"Yes, let's marry today then."

We walk towards the front of the room where Zeus is standing on the other side of the arbor as we go to stand underneath it. He holds a small golden bowl in his hands. Aphrodite stands to one side of the arbor and the girl I saw at the makeup store stands on the other side. "I know you," I say. "You helped me find Aphrodite's name."

"Is that how you got it? And you still remember what she looks like?" Eros asks. "Daughter, thank you for helping my love find her path. Janan, this is my daughter Hedone."

"Nice to meet you, Hedone."

"May all your days have bliss," she says.

Aphrodite says, "May your beauty never fade and you bear many children."

Zeus then says, "Do you come here willingly of your own accord?"

"I do," I answer.

"Do you take Eros to be your husband?"

"I do."

"Do you take Eros' family as your own?"

"I do."

"Do you take on the weight of power to use it sparingly and only when in need?'

"I do."

"Do you willingly accept the ambrosia in full knowledge of the danger?"

"I do."

"Then let us bind you to your fate."

Aphrodite and Hedone both take gold ribbons and tie them around our joined hands. Eros kisses me gently. Then pulls back to allow Zeus to come forward. "Take this ambrosia as a symbol of your new fate. Will what fate may bring be harmonious with the universe. May you live and grow power. May you become a god and look after the world in unison with fate. Take this ambrosia now and live forever." He places one piece of the ambrosia on my tongue and I eat it. He then gives me another piece to eat as well. "Now you have taken the required dosage of ambrosia, we shall wait and see what the fates will bring."

They unbound our hands and lead us to the bed. "Lie here until your test has passed," Aphrodite says. Eros and I sit down on the bed and the others leave the room. "Why didn't they ask you any questions? Like, are you willing to marry me?" I ask Eros.

"It's a given that I want you. This is more to make sure you are here of your own will and that you know the dangers. To protect you in case you were unsure. Only those brave enough and in love take the risk. If you only want to be a god and not have me, then you would not pass the test."

"How long does it take before you know I'm a god?"

"It takes a while, but if you have a negative reaction, we will see it soon. Over the next couple of hours, I will watch over you to see if you are ok. If there is no reaction after the first couple of hours, that's a good sign. You might just be a mortal who can take ambrosia, and that means you could live longer than normal. Or possibly you might turn into an immortal. Only time will tell."

"What should we do while we wait?" I ask with a silky tone.

"I like where you are headed, my lady," Eros says as he leans towards me, taking his hand to the side of my face and holding my head as he comes in for a kiss. We kiss as if there was no such thing as time, slowly and deeply. My hands are on his chest, feeling his muscles. I reach under his shirt and push it up and off of him. He grabs my butt and pulls me closer so that we fall onto the bed, with me laying on top of him. He pushes up my shirt, takes it off of me, and unhooks my bra. We both reach for our pants' zippers to unzip them next, along with our underwear. We are free and full of desire. Eros pulls me onto him again so that I am riding him. I push against him, feeling his desire, and it makes me wet. We kiss again with one hand on my breast and the other on my butt cheek. I push against him some more, then sit up so I can take him in. I slowly lower myself onto him. He feels magnificent, so filling, stretching me so wonderfully. Once he is all in, I squeeze my muscles around him, making him moan. I move up and down, watching his face as he calls out my name. Moving up and down squeezing my muscles, the friction of the movements feel really good, and I begin to feel light and full of pleasure. As the tension mounts, I move faster and faster until I come, leaking come on Eros. "You're so hot. You just came on me. That is such a turn on. Now it's my turn." He grabs my butt with his hands and moves quickly inside me with such force it makes me moan for more. We moan together as he suddenly becomes a little wider inside, then he comes deep inside me. It feels so good I keep riding him and a little longer is all I needed to come again. Then I fall onto him, weak in pleasure.

After a few moments, we pull apart and then I go to lie down beside him, cuddling into his side with his arm around me. We stay like that for a while in silence, basking in the pleasure we both just shared. I fall asleep feeling warm and happy.

Chapter 25

I wake up slowly, feeling warm, knowing Eros is still beside me. I open my eyes and smile at him. "Good morning, my lady. The morning sun is making you glow." He says.

"That's what I said to you," I laugh.

"Do you feel any different?"

"No, only very hot."

"Well, my dear, you are glowing with power. You have become a goddess. Did you not have any trouble last night as the Ambrosia went through your body? Sometimes, people have a difficult time. I knew your potential was great." He says as he pulls me in for a hug.

"I had a few moments of feeling like I was outside my body. It was strange. I could see us sleeping here, but couldn't do anything. I also saw the stars' and moon's rays full of color, inviting me up into the heavens. But feeling you nearby kept me grounded. Is that normal?"

"Yes, that's normal. I'm glad you didn't have any serious side effects. Having me help you feel grounded was a good thing. You might have flown away and not been able to come back to your body. That happens sometimes. We will have to train you to find and control your powers. You will need to say you're going on vacation until we can get you to stop glowing. It takes some practice. We will learn your powers as they develop. Everyone is different. But your powers will be linked to mine, so I will help you develop your powers. Where would you like to go on holiday?"

"I will have powers? That sounds fun and a little bit scary. What are your powers? Will we really go on vacation?"

"Yes, and yes. It's our honeymoon. We will get a private villa so that we have enough room and privacy needed to train you. And my powers are immortality, quick healing, flight from my wings, making someone fall in love or lust, or making someone immune to love."

"I've never been to Greece. I'd like to get to know your old home."

"Greece is perfect. I can show you all my old haunts, both ancient and modern. We can get a villa for a few weeks, then travel around once you can control your glow."

"That will be so much fun!'

"Also, I would like to marry you again with all our families and friends present."

"Really. That would be nice. I'd like to have my sister there when we marry."

"Of course. Your wish is my command, my lady."

"But what about work? I can't miss that much work."

"Luckily I'm the boss and can approve anything I wish," He winks at me.

Laughing with him, we hug some more. "I can get used to this," I say.

There is a knock on the door and Eros goes over to the door and opens it to find a cart with breakfast on it. He brings it in and puts the food on the bistro table at the side of the room. "Come, my lady, breakfast is served," he says.

I walk over and sit in one of the chairs. "Why do you call me 'My Lady'" I ask.

"Because I am your servant, your husband, who will worship you for all time," he answers.

"That's a nice thought. What endearment should I call you?"

"You can call me αγάπη μου (agApi mou). It means my love."

"Oh, how sweet. Thank you αγάπη μου."

As we eat our breakfast, we chat and laugh together. As we finish breakfast, we go to Eros' office to plan our trip. When we come in, Zeus, Aphrodite, and Hedone are waiting for us. "You have become a god! How wonderful!" Aphrodite says, "I welcome you gladly into this family. Sorry I was so negative, but I was worried you would not pass the test and Eros would be heartbroken all over again."

"Welcome Janan to our family," Hedone says.

Zeus looks pleased. "Welcome to godhood. We must talk about your responsibilities that come from being a god. But that can wait for another day. Today we celebrate our new god to the family."

"We are going on our honeymoon to Greece. We will have another wedding for our families once Janan has adapted to being a god," Eros says.

"Wonderful news," says Aphrodite.

"Janan and I will start planning it. We will have it at one of Dionysius' vineyards." Eros says, pulling my hand close to his chest, bringing me in for a kiss.

"Let's bring out the wine and ouzo," says Hedone.

We all gathered around the table to take our ouzo shot, "to love" Aphrodite says, "to love" we repeat and we all laugh and drink our shot. We had a great time celebrating together, for love has brought back Eros' soul, his psyche, his Janan. And they will live in harmony together forever.

Epilogue

THREE MONTHS LATER

I am nervous even though we are already married. Is it because there are so many people who have come to the wedding? So many mortals, gods, and other magical beings. I am waiting for my cue to go down the aisle with Eros' daughter Hedone and my sister Chloe, my bridesmaids who are by my side.

"You look stunning! You have since you fell in love, you glow happiness," Chloe says.

"You have no idea, but you see much," says Hedone to Chloe.

Finally, the music starts for me to go down the aisle. We line up and slowly make our way to the front, where Eros waits with his groomsmen. *Man, he looks hot in a suit.* Eros takes my hand from my sisters and we stand in front of the priest, staring at each other. We both grasp each other's hands with love. We see no one else, only each other, and barely hear the priest. This priest is special as she knows the truth about the gods and is a priest in the old ways but dressed like a catholic priest for the mortals as modern Greece worships a different god now. We are wed and have our first kiss as a married couple, and everyone cheers. As our kiss continues with our tongues down each other's throats, people hoot at us. Finally, we are married officially according to the mundane world, and I have no regrets. This is the man for me.

We make our way from the ceremony space to the reception area of the vineyard. This vineyard is one of many that Dionysus owns in Greece. He sponsored our wedding as he looks after Eros like a nephew. Dionysus seems a friendly and charismatic god. But he seems a little lonely when he talks to me and Eros while we wait for all the guests to make their way over to the reception area. His eyes watch one of his employees as she moves about serving the guests. The employee seems a bit annoyed at Dionysus and is avoiding him.

As Chloe goes over to get us some flutes of champagne, she goes over to that employee to take some flutes off her tray. They talk about the strange people at the wedding. I can over hear a bit of what they say.

"Is it just me, or does that guy have too much leg hair?" The employee says.

"Yes, he has a lot of hair. What about that guy who has wings glued to his sneakers? What cosplay is that?" Chloe asks.

"What about that woman and her shiny skin?" the employee says.

"Many people here are shiny." Chloe confirms.

"αγάπη μου, I think those two can see beyond the mist. We can have them tested." I say to Eros and Dionysus.

Dionysus looks pleased. "That works well for me. I'll see to testing my employee when the time is right."

"You were right. She has the same potential as you did," Eros says.

Chloe returns with the flutes of champagne. "You guys have some interesting guests. Is it normal for guests to cosplay at weddings?"

"We come as we are in all places. There are many types of people. Be careful not to say too much in case you offend anyone," Dionysus says as he walks over to talk to his employee.

"Oh, I didn't mean to offend anyone," Chloe says.

"Do not worry sister, you are with your family now. Just be yourself," I say.

Eros and I share a look of understanding and he bows his head in acceptance of testing my sister for godhood.

"Today is a day for new beginnings, sister," Eros says, "mingle and meet your family."

As Chloe walks away to join the crowd, Eros comes closer and whispers in my ear, "How would you like to practice your new powers?"

"Who would we practice on?"

"Well, let's look around and see if anyone stands out."

We look around the party for anyone who seems to need love. There are many people about, but one couple catches my attention. It was Dionysus and his employee. They are arguing still in a corner of the party, away from the rest of the group.

I lean over to Eros. "What about those two? I seem to remember his name from the private event that I helped set up some months ago. And she can see beyond the mist. They look like an old married couple already."

"Good choice. Here, take my bow and this arrow." He says as he passes me the bow and some arrows.

"Where did that come from? There was nothing here a moment ago."

"I can call it to me instantaneously when needed."

"Oh, that's handy. Will you teach me how to do that?"

"Of course. For now, let's practice shooting people. You should shoot Dionysus first. It will be harder to get the arrow to sink into the god than the mortal. Plus, Dionysus might need more time for it to take effect because of his past. Prepare your arrow, feel love, and let it fill the arrow."

"Ok," I say as I lift the arrow and bow. I aim for Dionysus, trying to focus on his broad back. I let out my breath and then shoot the arrow. It hit its mark. Dionysus freezes for a minute, then stares at his employee as she looks concerned over him. "Are you ok? Are you having a heart attack?" She asks Dionysus.

"Hurray, now shoot her," Eros commands.

I lift the bow once more with a new arrow. It is harder to aim for the employee, as she is behind Dionysus. I find her chest as Dionysus moves a little to the side. I shoot my arrow, and it hits her. She stops for a moment and stares at Dionysus. Both Dionysus and the employee stare at each other in wonder for a moment. They then continue arguing.

"Did I fail?" I ask Eros.

"Hmm, sometimes people are too stubborn. It may take a while to set in so we won't know if we failed or not for some time. Let's try another couple and see if it's easier than those two."

We look around the party once more. There were many people, but none seem to be suitable targets. But then Eros points out Hermes and Chloe, who were talking about his shoes. "I can't shoot my sister! She needs to find love naturally. I want her to find an everlasting love like I have with you. A true partnership."

"I think there is already a spark there for both of them. Maybe we can just shoot Hermes as gods fall in love with difficulty. Would you be alright with that, my lady?"

"Yes, I can shoot him. It will make me more comfortable if they date because he is already in love with her and he's not just playing around. I can trust that he won't abandon her." I aim my bow and arrow once more and shoot Hermes. He takes a deep breath and looks around, spotting me with the bow. He raises his hand in a wave and goes back to talking to Chloe.

"Did I fail again?" I ask Eros.

"That is definitely an unusual response," Eros agrees. "We shall wait and see for those two as well. Take heart, my lady, it is your first few shots of love. If it doesn't work, we will try again. Your magic might not be strong enough yet."

Eros and I return to the party and rejoin in celebrating our union once more with all of our loved ones. We party the entire night and have a giant breakfast the next morning. As the start of my new life as an immortal with powers is overwhelming, I am ready to see what adventures will come up as I work beside my love, helping people and gods find their own love and happiness.

Get a Free Short Story

Join my newsletter to get a free short story of how Eros meet Janan before The Matchmaker.

When you join my newsletter you will get a free short story and an email newsletter once a month about my writing journey, books I'm reading, and a short introduction to a Greek mythological creature.
Join my newsletter here:
www.roxannegardener.com

About the Author

As a typical librarian, I love books! And I love stories about the Ancient Greek Gods and Heroes. Putting these two loves together I decided to write about Greek mythology in a contemporary fashion.

instagram.com/roxannegardenerdesigns/

pinterest.com/roxannegardener/

www.ingramcontent.com/pod-product-compliance
Lightning Source LLC
LaVergne TN
LVHW041642060526
838200LV00040B/1678